A THREE-TIERED PASTEL DREAM

A Three-Tiered Pastel Dream

STORIES

Lesley Trites

ESPLANADE BOOKS
THE FICTION IMPRINT AT VÉHICULE PRESS

Published with the generous assistance of the Canada Council for the Arts, the Canada Book Fund of the Department of Canadian Heritage, and the Société de développement des entreprises culturelles du Québec (SODEC).

Funded by the Government of Canada
Financé par le gouvernement du Canada | Canadä

Esplanade Books editor: Dimitri Nasrallah
Cover design: David Drummond
Photo of author: Alex Tran
Typeset in Minion and Futura by Simon Garamond
Printed by Marquis Printing Inc.

LIBRARY AND ARCHIVES CANADA CATALOGUING IN PUBLICATION

Trites, Lesley, author
A three-tiered pastel dream : stories / Lesley Trites.

Issued in print and electronic formats.
ISBN 978-1-55065-464-6 (SOFTCOVER). – ISBN 978-1-55065-471-4 (EPUB)

I. Title.

PS8639.R58T47 2017   C813'.6   C2016-907354-8
C2016-907355-6

Published by Véhicule Press, Montréal, Québec, Canada
vehiculepress.com

Distributed in Canada by LitDistCo
Distributed in the U.S. by Independent Publishers Group

Printed in Canada on FSC•certified paper.

CONTENTS

Pepto-Bismol Pink

Paula wakes to an empty bed, an empty room, a throbbing forehead. She looks at the bedside table, then the desk, but their surfaces are untouched. No note. She dresses quickly. Her hands shake as she swipes the tube across her lips. She's about to leave the hotel room when she glimpses her reflection in the mirror. She almost doesn't recognize herself. All she can see is the lipstick, the same colour she'd been wearing last night, a shade that now reminds her of Pepto-Bismol. She wipes it off and sees herself re-emerge in the mirror.

By 8 A.M. she's in the hotel lobby listening attentively to her boss' briefing, to his demands and requests. Her hands steady as they shuffle paper. By midday, last night's spell has dissipated, morning fog blown away by daylight.

If this were the '70s they would call her a career girl, charitably, because she doesn't have much of a career. She's always put her whole self into any administrative position she could get. She is the keeper of calendars, storage keys, room bookings, office holiday party plans, secrets. The first one in and the last one out. She excels at tracking the details no one else wants to pay attention to, is known for her meticulous spreadsheets with their advanced formulas. Her facility with Excel amazes even the accountants.

Knowledge is power, she tells herself, and some day she would have both.

Back at the office, she keeps busy, pushing away thoughts of Greg, the birthmark on his lower back, his soft hands. If she closes her eyes, she can still feel his touch. She tries to keep her eyes open at all times, attracting strange looks from colleagues.

When she starts gaining weight, Paula ignores it. Her weight has always fluctuated. But she's getting ready for work one morning, horizontal on the bed trying to do up her pants, when the button pops. She lies back and thinks. Her last period? She calls in sick, something she's never done before, and trudges to the pharmacy. She worries about who will unlock the meeting rooms, whether anyone will need office supplies in her absence.

It takes more than a few episodes of *Sex and the City,* episodes she's seen so many times she can recite the dialogue, before she can open the package containing the magic wand. She faces the two pink lines in the display window, gets up. Makes an omelette with red peppers and mushrooms, like she does every evening, but tonight she omits her customary glass of wine. She's unsettled by this omission, a seemingly small change in her daily routine. She can't get to sleep that night and blames it on the lack of wine.

She's back at work the next day, unlocking the supply cabinets before anyone else arrives. When no one's around she turns the key in the lock, back and forth. The swoosh and click of metal against metal is soothing. She slides her earbuds in and listens to "Singin' in the Rain" on repeat. She tries to ignore the people who float by her desk, the women who linger, wanting someone to listen to their gossip.

Some of these women are nice to Paula. Almost friends. They occasionally take her to lunch. But when it comes to Friday and Saturday and Sunday nights, everyone is busy with husbands, families, dogs. The lunches are pleasant, but the conversation floats at surface level. Sometimes someone takes an interest, tries to usher her into a new yoga or skincare regime, a juice fast, a spinning studio, a speed-dating event, an improv group, a salsa or pottery class—anything to shake her out of her quiet existence. She deflects this attention, smiling demurely.

She wears the same five outfits to work each week, sensible business casual skirts and shirts, the same pattern from Monday to Friday. Why change when she knows what she likes? Besides, she hates shopping. So at first she avoids buying new clothes to accommodate her growing belly. But eventually she's forced to buy a few pairs of pants, ugly things with elastic waistbands. When her stomach bulges past even the baggy peasant blouses and she's filled with nausea while picking at a Waldorf salad, she finally confesses to the two colleagues she trusts most, Anita and Gloria. They don't seem surprised. They continue sipping lemon iced tea, eating beet salads. They inquire about the father, in a gentle, roundabout way. She is evasive, in a gentle, roundabout way.

She keeps her speech minimal, practical. She's always had a hard time talking about herself, bringing thoughts from head to lips. She's happiest at home, alone, when she can kick off her heels, peel away her pantyhose and skirt. She hates the feel of fabric against skin. Not having anyone looking at her is a blessing.

She tries to get used to the flood of feeling that comes with being pregnant. The feelings aren't all positive, but they're hers, and she holds them in greedily. A new tenderness toward her body, a better reason for self-care. The mild nausea, really not so bad, that gives her license to consume ginger candy by the pound. She extends this allowance to weekly, and eventually daily, bowls of ice cream. She doesn't force herself to the gym, taking long bubble baths instead. Even the worry, about how she'll take care of this being on her own, is tinged with a tingling warmth that begins on the surface of her skin and goes deep into her core.

She never imagined having children, so there's a blank slate where some women's perfect child would be. She's old to be a mother, considered high risk at 39. At her first ultrasound, the doctor finds a fibroid behind her uterus. Cysts, too. It shouldn't affect the pregnancy. But the doctor's voice doesn't have as much confidence as Paula would like.

"It's a small miracle you got pregnant at all."

For once, Paula can read between the lines. Don't get too attached. As her belly grows bigger, she skirts questions, well-meaning lunch invitations to introduce her to other pregnant women, Anita's attempt to throw a shower. Months of pregnancy pass quickly, life as usual. But when she's eight months pregnant, frequent kicks announcing the baby's presence, she finally allows herself to dream. At home, she quietly prepares the room. She paints the walls pink.

She's in bed when her water breaks. She gets up, throws the sheets in the wash, calls a taxi. She's waiting on the front steps when the contractions start. Her body moving, rolling. She closes her eyes and rolls with it. Into the taxi, into the hospital waiting room, into her private room. All the way through the delivery. The pinprick of the epidural feels very, very far away, as if in another body entirely. The pain, the lights, the flurry of activity around her almost undoes her. She closes her eyes and separates herself from her body, as she's learned to do. When the doctor tells her to push, she focuses on the stethoscope, the way the light gleams off it, and loses herself in it until she feels a hand on her arm and a voice telling her she can stop.

"Isn't there someone you want us to call?" the nurse asks.

Paula shakes her head. Her eyes are on the baby, her fingers outstretched to caress cheeks, nose, ears, forehead.

The being that emerged from her. She's perfect.

It's hip to give girls names traditionally reserved for boys, she's learned, and so she names her Gregory. It's months before she makes the connection to why she chose this name.

Once they're allowed to leave the hospital and go home, Paula doesn't want anyone else to intrude. This is their time, hers and Gregory's. They would do this together, floating in the cozy cocoon that is Paula's apartment, now theirs. In the Pepto-Bismol pink room, where everything is calm. Where Gregory sleeps, coos, and flaps her tiny arms. Gregory is an unusually sweet and amicable baby. Such a happy camper. She sleeps through the night almost immediately, so regularly it's almost alarming. She coos instead of crying. She always has a smile on her face.

Paula doesn't miss life at the office. Motherhood. Did she really almost miss out on this? She had no idea she was capable of generating so much love for another being.

She won't compare Gregory to other children. She doesn't want to know about milestones, about measurements, about minimums and maximums. She only wants to know about her baby, in every last detail. So she observes her very carefully. One day Gregory kicks her leg to an imaginary rhythm, precise like a metronome. A musician? Another day she stretches up into a little backbend. A gymnast? Later, Paula wonders how she didn't notice anything was wrong, in these days of intense, quiet observation.

Sometimes Paula looks for signs of Greg, at least what she remembers of Greg, in Gregory. Greg's features are fuzzy when she tries to call them to mind. Maybe Gregory has some of his mannerisms, but she'll never know. She still thinks of him sometimes. He was the last man she'd been with, and she feels a strange, unfamiliar flush of embarrassment whenever she recalls it. Where had it come from, that connection? It lasted only a night, hadn't even made it past midnight.

Gregory is six months old when something seems to tighten inside of her. Something of interest, apparently, for it draws her deep into herself. Her face screws up in displeasure, her rosy complexion now shades of red and blue to match her howls. The pleasant cooing decreases and then ceases until Gregory spends her time in silence. Her eyes won't meet Paula's, even when she's breastfeeding, and she recoils from Paula's touch. The two of them spend all their time together in a three-room apartment, feeding and napping and bathing in a repetitive loop, so the difference is impossible not to notice. Paula doesn't understand why she can't reach her.

Paula tries everything. She sits in front of Gregory, using different tones of voice, even angry ones, to see if something will get her to respond. She buys as many toys as she can afford, taking Gregory on trips to Babies "ʀ" Us, hoping she'll express interest in something amid the colourful displays. But the bright lights and sounds only seem to cause Gregory to withdraw further into herself, and she ignores all the toys Paula puts in front of her.

"Mama," Paula says, pointing to her chest.

Gregory's eyes move with an imaginary tide, refusing to focus. Paula falls asleep on the floor and wakes up in a panic. Gregory is still sitting, silent. Paula gives up, lets tears spill. Gregory reaches her chubby little hand to Paula's cheek, then quickly takes it away. It happens so fast Paula wonders if she imagined it, but she feels hopeful until the next terrible tantrum. For by now Gregory is either silent or screeching, nothing in between.

In the grocery store Paula straps Gregory into the cart and she seems fine until she's screaming like a banshee. Assaults of accusing eyes, question marks and exclamation points burrow into Paula's skin like ticks. Paula abandons the groceries, orders takeout. Again. Always Thai. Taking Gregory out in public becomes so difficult she simply stops.

The screaming gets louder and goes on longer, until Paula hears it even when it's not there. Her landlord calls to tell her the neighbours have been complaining. Can't she do something? But she can't. Nothing works. Picking Gregory up only makes things worse. Every diaper change is such an ordeal that Paula tries to hold off as long as possible, preferring to bear the smell. She's forced to give up on breastfeeding. Her inability to comfort her own baby makes Paula feel the worst kind of hopelessness. What kind of mother is she? One day Gregory screams for twelve hours straight. Paula is not equipped for this. But, surprisingly, her love only grows stronger. She feels Gregory's pain like it's her own.

The end of her maternity leave comes and goes. She can't fathom going back to work, leaving Gregory in the hands of a stranger who wouldn't understand. But the money. Of course it's a problem.

One morning Paula can't face another call from the landlord, so she straps Gregory into a little-used stroller and heads out the door. It's spring, the snow almost melted. She pushes Gregory along a bumpy sidewalk, one not yet repaired from the ravages of winter, and she's around the corner before she finally notices it. The silence. Gregory isn't screaming. In fact, she makes cooing sounds each time they go over a bump. The longer they walk, the more Paula's body relaxes, the warmer she feels as she looks at her daughter, so pretty out here in this slanted light. Maybe it was just a phase?

The screams aren't continual anymore, but they come back at surprising times. Desperate for a shower, Paula keeps Gregory strapped into the car seat and sets it in the corner of the bathroom. She leaves the shower curtain drawn back so she can watch Gregory while she shampoos. She emerges in a hurry. The wails start, and they don't quiet down until Paula's hair is dry again.

It's change, Paula finally realizes. Gregory doesn't like it. That's normal, isn't it? Being averse to change? Many people are. She is. And how overwhelming and confusing the world must seem for someone so small, so new to everything. Maybe Gregory is just exquisitely sensitive, attuned to the world at an unusual frequency.

It's by accident that Paula discovers something else that helps. When she can manage it, now that they go for daily walks, Paula stops and treats herself to a Berry Banana smoothie at the shop down the street, a colourful place that serves calorie-laden drinks with bright purple straws. Gregory grabs at the straw, so Paula passes it to her. She is enthralled for the next hour, running it over her lips. Paula is relieved, yet uneasy, so focused Gregory seems on this object, a piece of plastic. But soon she takes this out whenever she can, passing Gregory a straw whenever she needs to keep her occupied. She stuffs a few extra into her purse every time she buys a smoothie, feeling her face flush as she does so, wondering if one of the employees will eventually notice and say something.

Paula had naively believed that babies need stimulation, change, diversion, but she learns that if she and Gregory stick to a predictable routine, things go much smoother. She learns how to listen to her not-yet-verbal daughter, to pay attention to the signs, watch her body language. She learns how to tune in to Gregory's frequency, and Gregory even begins to smile again. They walk to the smoothie shop each morning, Gregory cooing in her stroller. They stop at the park on the way home. She plops Gregory into a baby swing and pushes her, ever so gently. Gregory flaps her hands in delight.

Rainy days are horrible for both of them. Signals get scrambled.

Sometimes Paula feels her daughter has been locked away, and if she could just find the key, the right key, she could let her out. Or, maybe, let herself in. Into Gregory's world. Gregory often stares at the calendar on the fridge, as if trying to discern its pattern. Like she's taking note of the appointments listed there, though she doesn't yet speak. So Paula decides to start with this. She takes the calendar down from the wall and starts reading it to Gregory like it's a book: month, day, number, appointment.

Gregory doesn't respond, exactly, but she also doesn't try to escape from Paula's lap. She sits still and seems focused.

Encouraged, Paula keeps trying. She holds up cards and pronounces the words carefully, slowly, over and over. Cat. Mouse. Dog. Bird. Gregory keeps looking away, at the overhead lamp, the wallpaper, anything but Paula's face. But Paula persists. After a couple weeks of this, she's rewarded with eye contact. That's when she knows she must continue. Paula adds new cards to the deck. Gregory doesn't show much interest until they get to the butterfly card. Then, she's enthralled, reaching up to trace the outline of its wings. Gregory becomes fascinated with the butterflies in her new colouring book, tracing them over and over with her crayons until Paula can barely see the original black lines.

The difficult moments haven't disappeared. Paula comes very close to losing her cool one morning when Gregory throws a tantrum because they're out of Rice Krispies, the only cereal she'll eat. But now that she's seeing progress, Paula finds it easier to persevere.

"Fuck a duck," Gregory says one morning.

Paula gasps. Two wordless years, and now this. She hadn't realized how closely Gregory had been listening. She learns to be more careful with her words, even when Gregory seems lost in her own world. Those three words unleash something and now Gregory begins speaking. No baby talk for her: full sentences.

"Want smoothie," she says, when they're late one day leaving for their daily walk.

"Gregory wants a straw," Paula says.

"Gregory wants a straw," Gregory repeats.

Her speech comes slowly, then quickly, in floods.

They spend more and more time curled up on the couch, reading. Many books about butterflies. The idea that caterpillars can transform into butterflies is of endless interest to Gregory.

"Again," she says, when Paula closes the book.

Soon, Gregory can identify many different types of butter-flies.

"Painted Lady," she says, caressing the wings of the butter-fly in her book. "Giant Swallowtail."

Butterflies can't hear, Gregory tells Paula. They feel. They taste with their feet. Gradually, Paula realizes Gregory is repeating what she hears around her. Like a butterfly, Gregory is adept at mimicry, at least when it comes to speech. But hard as Paula tries, Gregory won't address her as Mama, or by any name at all. And Paula still has to dress Gregory in the morning, brush her teeth at night.

Anita comes to visit. She brings a stuffed rabbit, but Gregory refuses to look at it or Anita. Gregory does not react well to strangers in the house. She goes about it gently, as is her style, but Anita wants to know if Paula would consider taking Gregory to see someone. Just to see. Paula makes tea.

Anita never gives up. She never stops coming, never stops bringing toys despite Gregory's lack of interest. And one day, finally, she is rewarded. She brings a small spinning top, wooden, old fashioned. Gregory still doesn't look at Anita, but she grabs the top and spins it. She is still spinning when Anita leaves, happy with herself. On her way out Anita presses a business card into Paula's hand.

Paula leaves the business card on the kitchen table and tries to ignore it. A presence emerges from it, filling the kitchen, seeping into the bedroom and finally Gregory's room until it has contaminated the entire apartment. Paula can't take it anymore. She needs to exorcise this suffocating presence, and so she finally calls the number on the card. The appointment made, the card's power is diffused. It becomes simply a piece of card stock with embossed black lettering again.

Paula takes Gregory to the address on the card, tasting the dread filling her stomach. Acrid. In the doctor's office she tries to explain, but it doesn't come out right. How can she sum up a person, a personality? Gregory will soon be three years old.

The official diagnosis falls like the blow of a hammer. How can this doctor be so sure? Some of the things the doctor describes don't seem unusual to Paula. Being extremely sensitive to sound, to visual stimulation, to bright colours and lights, to the textures of food. Inflexible to changes in routine. Strong attachment to unusual objects. Paula can relate. But then there are the important things, the diagnostic ones, he says: lack of imaginative play, difficulties with communication and social relationships. What it seems to come down to is that Gregory won't look the doctor in the eye, won't in fact acknowledge his presence at all.

Paula vows to get a second opinion. The second doctor offers the same diagnosis, but her suggestions are different. She tells Paula about the various therapies available, suggests books to read, steps to take, therapists to call.

"Most importantly," she says, "find some support. You'll need it."

Paula tells herself this doesn't change anything: she refuses to let it define either of them. She doesn't want this new label to blot out her Gregory, everything she's learned about her so far. She doesn't want this to upset the world she has carefully crafted for the two of them, a safe place where they can both be comfortable. She cannot bear to have Gregory categorized, a butterfly with its wings pinned to a bulletin board, like those she saw on the top floor of that creepy taxidermy store. Gregory is still beautifully free, unhinged. Why should she be tamed, caught under a glass jar?

Paula hates the word spectrum, how it sounds so science-like without the comfort of precision. And too much like speculum. Cold. But the word creeps into her life, insidious. Later, she finds refuge in this word. It's a spectrum, Paula reminds herself, and hopes that Gregory is at one end of it.

She goes online and reads about geniuses on the spectrum. A California man whose illuminating music criticism wins him a Pulitzer. An animal behavioural consultant and professor, a woman *Time* names a hero in their list of influential people. A singer-songwriter who makes pure, confident yet vulnerable pop music, songs about anxiety. A contestant on "America's Next Top Model." A young man in London who recites pi from memory for five hours, like it's a poem, each number containing and expressing emotion. Paula's eyes brim with a dangerous hope that inflates and soothes a part of her that may later be slashed and dashed.

She recalls how, as a girl, she took comfort inside numbers, tracing them over and over in her notebook as if she were writing in a diary. To her, numbers had been personal. She'd cover her page with her arm in case her classmates spied, not wanting them to decode her. She wants to help Gregory find comfort, find herself. She reads all the books the doctor recommends, learns about different therapies, debates and controversies, lingo. She begins to formulate a plan.

But, the money. It's going to have to come from somewhere. Therapy costs money, after all. Lots of it. Time is not on her side. There's a window, the doctors tell her, and it's closing. Gregory needs more than Paula can give her. Hours of therapy, personal attention. Her insurance will only take her so far.

Does Greg have money? She combs her memory for signs. Non-profit. No, maybe not. But he had been wearing a suit. He must make a decent salary. She has no interest in contacting him. Thinking about him is different from actually having to engage with him. She prefers to keep him in memory, an object for fantasy. When she first found out she was pregnant, of course the panic set in. But it had subsided surprisingly quickly, and she never considered involving him. To her, it didn't seem like any of his business. He hadn't even left a note, after all. But now, things are different.

She still has his business card. She'd taken it from the stack she'd found in his shirt pocket, along with a silver ring that looked suspiciously like a wedding band, when he'd been in the bathroom that night. It's been tucked into the corner of the mirror above her dresser this whole time. Now it's splattered with stray drops of the fig and vanilla perfume she's had for years. She doesn't like to spray it directly on her body but sometimes she puffs it into the air and walks through the cloud.

She plucks the card out. The part hidden behind the frame of the mirror is whiter than the rest. She puts it on top of her keyboard, where it sits for a few days. She avoids the internet altogether while she tries to wrestle up the courage. But she can't bear the thought of sending an email and waiting; she needs his immediate reaction. She'll have to call. Each time she looks at Gregory, she knows she has to do it. This is the only way. It's already getting late. The doctors stress the need for early intervention.

"Hello?"

His voice jars her. So different from the voice in her mind, the one that has been whispering to her in the night these past few years. The voice of a stranger. So foreign, in fact, that she almost hangs up. But she looks at Gregory, who is busy playing with her tiny alphabet magnets, composing them into words only she understands. Paula takes a deep breath.

"You may not remember me. It's been a l-l-long time."

Oh, god, not the stuttering. Something she tried so hard to get over as a teenager, practicing in front of the mirror until she could say "Hello, how are you?" without flubs.

The phone receiver feels hard and cold against her ear. Silence on the other end.

"It's P-P-Paula. We met at the bar at Hotel Europa."

"Paula," he says.

She can't tell from his tone whether he remembers. She hears noise in the background, people talking. Of course, he's at work. What was she thinking?

"You bought me a martini," she says.

"I remember you. Hold on, let me go somewhere a little quieter," he says.

When he picks up again, the background noise is gone.

"I'm back."

Paula closes her eyes and forces herself to utter the words, feeling light-headed.

"A child?" he says. "Are you sure?"

"Quite sure."

"No, I mean, are you sure the child is mine?"

"There's no doubt."

"Wow. Well…"

"I know it wasn't your choice to bring a child into the world. I never intended to contact you, it's just that…"

"Just that what?"

"Gregory is special."

"Gregory?"

"Yes."

"Huh. What do you mean, special?"

"Sorry, that's not the right way to say it."

"You mean he…"

"She, actually."

"She? You named our daughter Gregory?"

"My daughter. Yes, I named my daughter Gregory."

He is silent for a minute.

"Special how?"

She tries to explain, about the doctors and their theories. About early intervention.

"Autism," he says. "Wow."

This word hangs between them for a few seconds.

"I see," he continues quietly. "So this is about money."

"Well, yes."

"So she's not my daughter but you want my money."

"It's not like that."

"What's it like?"

"What do you know about it?" she asks.

"I saw a documentary once."

She sighs.

"I know, everyone probably talks about some movie they saw."

Actually, she doesn't know, because she's only discussed Gregory with doctors.

"What would you rather they say?" he asks.

She's never thought about this.

"I…I guess I'd rather they ask what she's like. What she likes."

"What does Gregory like?"

"She loves butterflies. She can identify about a hundred different species by now. She also loves dogs, at least from afar. Purple straws. Puzzles. She's memorized the timetable of the bus stop outside our apartment, so she can always tell me when the next bus is coming, which is useful, even if we never take the bus."

When they hang up, she collapses onto the couch, still shaking. She lets out her breath, leans back into the cushions and laughs. She did it.

Days pass. Nothing. No emails. She begins to regret putting herself out there like that. She's never been good at dealing with people when emotions are involved. She can deal with people who want to order office supplies or book meeting rooms. Practical, easy things where she doesn't have to read their minds, their faces, their emotions. Why did she think this would be different?

But what can she do? She's not going to call him again. She has to wait. She's also going to have to face facts. What will happen to her and Gregory if he doesn't give her money? She can't get a job, leave Gregory with someone else. Anyone equipped to handle Gregory would need to be paid more or as much as Paula would make.

They go to the park on the first real day of spring, the day everyone is unwinding their scarves and unzipping their jackets, holding them over their arms. Gregory is hesitant at first, squinting up at the sun, but as they sit on a bench, Paula sees her relax. After a while Gregory approaches a nearby tree, one with big roots. Spontaneously, she throws her arms around it. Paula closes her eyes for a moment, enjoying the sun, the peaceful feeling, Gregory's happiness. When she opens them Gregory is spinning in a circle, closed eyes up toward the sky, her chaotic blond curls bouncing. Paula has never seen her look so happy.

When they get home, Paula finds an unmarked package on their doorstep. Inside is a butterfly puzzle. Gregory spends hours on it.

When the phone rings, Paula eyes it suspiciously. She's accustomed to its silence.

She's surprised to hear Greg's voice. He must have taken her number from call display, used it to find her address. She still uses a landline with an old answering machine; she forgets about people with their cell phones, easily displayed numbers, how vulnerable you make yourself by calling someone. She hates that, being available to people. It's why she doesn't have a cell phone, why she tries to avoid giving out her email address, why she never signs in to online chat. Being online so people can talk to her by clicking a button makes her feel like a raw nerve. When it pings, she jumps.

"Tell me about her," Greg says.

Where to start?

"She has blonde curls," she says.

"Like you."

"My hair is brown."

"Oh, sorry."

"Green eyes. A smile that's rare but angelic when it does appear."

"Go on."

"The other day she petted a dog for the first time. Progress. A golden lab."

"Maybe she'd want a puppy."

"Oh, god, no!"

She's trying hard to be amenable to Greg's request for details, but her bodily rejection of this idea is instinctual. Is he crazy?

"Sorry, I just…"

"Gregory is enough to handle."

"I understand. I know it must be…I was just trying…"

"It's okay," she says.

"I haven't spent much time around kids," he says. "I'm not sure what I'm supposed to do, here."

"You're not supposed to do anything," she says, although of course that's not what she means.

Greg's help comes in the mail. With his cheque in hand, she calls the therapist, the one the doctor recommended.

Time speeds up after that. Everything happens so fast. They go from being a quiet team, mother and daughter, to a team of specialists. Their small apartment is taken over by therapists, by meetings, by special toys and binders of information. Paula often has to close her eyes and take deep breaths, adjusting to the presence of other people in their space. But soon she is heading up a small army, behavioural and speech therapists. She is calling the school board about finding a place for Gregory. She is trying to suck everything she can out of her insurance company. She can't imagine returning to work.

Mothering Gregory is a full-time job. She does reach points, every so often, when she doesn't think she can do it anymore. Not alone. Not like this. But she can't give up on Gregory. Of course she can't.

To have a child who won't hug or kiss her, who won't address her as Mama but only as "you" feels like dashed hopes. Most of the time, she knows her daughter isn't trying to hurt her. But sometimes she forgets. Sometimes she doubts. Sometimes she thinks Gregory is doing it on purpose. Sometimes she doesn't know what to think. Sometimes she goes to a very dark place, looking at Gregory. There are moments when she has no patience left, when her hands clench together and she worries that someday they might clench the wrong thing. Gregory's arm, for instance, when she won't look at Paula, when she ignores her.

The therapists tell her she needs a firmer tone of voice, a firmer hand. She needs to dispense with indulgence. This approach is not about being pleasant and supportive, they explain. You need to become your child's teacher. You need to interrupt her routine. Paula has never been a good teacher, was never assertive or authoritative enough. She feels each failure in repressed tears that make her temples throb.

Greg calls again, asks how things are going.

"Do you really want to know?"

"Of course."

"I'm the most exhausted I've ever been in my life. But I think it's helping."

Paula tries again to paint a charming portrait of Gregory for him: her lily skin, her chubby cherub legs, her occasional outbursts of pure glee. The effort is exhausting. She wants to talk about something else, for a change.

So he tells her what he remembers of that night: her blue dress, that stretchy material, the way it felt under his hand as he guided her into the backseat of a cab. Her hair to her shoulders, the way she nervously twirled a strand of it around her finger as she spoke. A fluorescent pink outline of a palm tree in a window and the Thai place that served curry in coconuts and lemongrass daiquiris with festive umbrellas. He admits that when she went to the washroom, he asked the waiter to make his dish less spicy.

"You were easy to talk to," he says, "so unassuming. Quiet."

"That I am," she says. "Quiet is usually the first word used to describe me."

"The women in my family are so loud. Sometimes having a therapist for a mother is too much pressure, you know? Like every conversation has to be so meaningful. So I clam up around her in protest."

"Didn't you say your mother was a sex therapist?"

"Yes, right. But being a therapist permeates her whole personality. She can't seem to talk to anyone without imagining they're on the couch."

Paula and Greg don't discuss meeting. They don't discuss finances, or even, after a while, Gregory. Yet their conversations become frequent, then daily. She hears the clink of ice cubes in his glass and asks what he's drinking. Gin and tonic. The next day she ducks Gregory into the liquor store and buys herself a pint of gin. She pours herself a companionable gin and tonic in the evenings, once Gregory is in bed, and waits for his call. The conversation lasts the length of the drink, which she sips more and more slowly. Falling into a rhythm. It's always him who calls, once he gets home from work.

"What were you afraid of when you were a kid?" he asks.

"Oh, god, everything." She laughs. "Garden snakes, spiders, God, death, marshmallow fluff, skeletons, sliced black olives, dogs."

"But not cats?"

"No. I didn't like how dogs were so forward, so affectionate, so full of emotion. I couldn't understand them. Too eager. That scared me. Cats, on the other hand, kept to themselves. I could observe them from a distance. I liked how elegant and still they seemed. Still, at least, until they streaked across the street. So decisive."

"Huh. I had a cat as a kid, but I never liked her that much. She wasn't very cuddly."

"And you? What were you afraid of?" she asks.

He thinks for a minute.

"Scarves," he says.

"Scarves?"

"My mother always wore a scarf when I was young, until one day when I was about five, when her scarf got caught in the escalator at the department store. We'd been on our way to look at pillowcases. The scarf tightened around her neck, and she fell down before someone helped her unwind it. I watched it disappear into the dark machinery of the stairs as we stood there and moved up the escalator. She was sad because she'd bought it in Paris on her honeymoon."

"I'd have thought that would have given you a fear of escalators."

"Well, that too. I always take the stairs."

She can feel him gradually opening up to her, telling her more and more as time passes. He's not especially happy in his career. He chose finance because it seemed sensible, because business was where everyone he knew headed when it was time to go to university. But when he got into the field he hated it, alienated by the competitive atmosphere. So he'd switched into non-profit, where the salaries were smaller but his business skills and financial knowledge were valued, where he felt like he was contributing to something that might actually make a difference. But now he feels belittled and restricted by the board of directors.

"Do you regret the past?"

Her drink is almost finished when he asks.

"Doesn't everyone?"

"I don't think so, not everyone."

"I don't like to think about what I can't change," she says.

This isn't entirely true, but she likes how it makes her sound strong, resolute.

"I regret lots of things."

He sighs so loudly she can almost feel his breath through the phone.

"I knew I would regret it, if I didn't help you, with Gregory," he says. "I knew it would gnaw at me, having a daughter I knew nothing about."

"I still haven't told you that much about her."

"I know. But I'm getting to know her through her mother."

"Maybe you'd want to … meet her?"

He doesn't answer. She hears him shuffling, a noise in the background, a woman's voice. He says he's sorry but he has to go.

She hangs up the phone, finishes her drink, regrets.

The next night Paula collapses into an armchair, waiting, ice cubes in glass, but he doesn't call. She watches Gregory

31

on the other side of the room. Gregory refused to go to sleep and now she's reassembling her butterfly puzzle with a focus Paula can't help but admire. She has circles under her eyes, though, and Paula wonders how the hours of therapy are affecting her, how much they're really helping. What if it's only making things worse, forcing Gregory to conform against her nature? But, the experts. They must know what they're doing. Paula tries not to think about causation. She can't handle the thought that she might somehow be responsible for inflicting this on her daughter, genetically or otherwise. She tries to focus on the present, what she can do in the here and now.

She sits down in front of Gregory.

"Do you want Mama to help you with that?"

Gregory doesn't look at her.

"Mama," she tries again, pointing to her chest. "Gregory," she continues, pointing to Gregory.

Her effort is half-hearted; she's listening for the phone. These evening conversations with Greg have become small islands of reprieve from her daily schedule, the only chance she has for real, engaged conversation. Her lifeline. Never has she been able to talk to someone this way. The distance helps. She doesn't have to worry about eye contact or body language; she can just focus on the sound of his voice.

Still no phone call.

Old-fashioned phone conversations can be more intimate than sex, she reads in a magazine.

Two more days and she caves, calls him. He apologizes but doesn't explain.

This time, he wants to know what she remembers.

The attractiveness of his two-day stubble, his wearied evening look and how it reminded her of the white creases in her favourite pair of jeans. His weekend suit despite the heat, later thrown across the back of a chair in her room. How he didn't point out the lipstick on her teeth. His casual confidence. His white teeth. The way he caressed her softly, from head to shoulder to hip to toe, almost like she was a cat, one he was fond of. The soothing way he spoke during sex. She leaves these last details out.

"Where do you feel happiest?" she asks.

"In a canoe."

This surprises her.

He tells her about the week he spent canoe camping, totally alone. Sometimes he'd lie back in the canoe and float, watching the clouds drift past, sipping a beer.

"Those were my happiest times," he says. "Before..."

And that's when he lets it slip, that word that changes their dynamic. Wife. Until now they haven't acknowledged her existence. Paula hasn't wanted to think about it. But once it's out he can't seem to control the torrent that follows, and now Paula can't avoid it.

She has a name: Nicole. He met her online years ago. First date tumbled into cohabitation into ring shopping. She made it easy for him, hints about carat size, setting, and band material, a mention of her ring size dropped into casual conversation. An architect who works long hours, who arrives home late after he's prepared dinner. He enjoys cooking. A soothing ritual. Lately, though, sometimes Nicole comes home and dinner still isn't ready.

His wife doesn't want children, never has.

"Do you?" she asks.

33

"I never thought I did," he says.

She breaks an unwritten rule by pouring a second drink. And that's what allows her to suggest it again. A meeting.

They agree on a time and a place. The next day, the park. He'll play hooky, leave early, drive over to meet them.

She doesn't sleep that night. Gregory senses something is unusual when they leave the house the next day. She screams as they head toward the park, and Paula wonders what she's got them both into, what line she's crossed.

But it's all for nothing, because they sit in the park all day. Alone. Just the two of them. Finally she has to take Gregory home.

That night, she lets the phone ring. It rings and rings, until finally she takes it off the hook.

A cheque arrives. She doesn't cash it. She swears off gin.

Gregory is in the park, playing beside the other children. Paula watches from a park bench, a novel on her knees. She doesn't know why she bothered bringing it, because she can't take her eyes off Gregory long enough to read. She flips it over and looks at the back cover. A thriller.

He's there before she notices him, a big boy, strong hands, looming over her delicate daughter. A truck in his hand, poised to strike.

"Mama," screams Gregory.

Tears in Paula's eyes at the sound. She runs to her.

"Mama," Gregory says again.

"Mama's here," Paula says. "Mama's here."

But that truck.

That night, the phone rings. She has no choice. This time, she picks it up.

A Three-Tiered Pastel Dream

Mara, I won't say some day you'll understand, because you likely never will.

I've been denying my curiosity all these years like an anorexic teen who won't admit she wants that fucking cupcake, my life a game of not thinking about you, of avoiding all the sidewalk's cracks. But about a month ago I felt something deep within snap to attention, a physical, painful crack of the spine but also a deep quiver shooting up the lightning rod of my psyche. That's when I knew that you were trying to reach me. But of course you wouldn't know how. So I slip-soled up the steps of the library determined to harness that beast, the internet, and find you.

The old chair creaked under my weight as the Google logo winked at me. I'd used computers back in my days at the hospital, of course, but that was well before the internet took over. To me the internet was still vast, vague, unknowable. But my colleagues had explained it to me, the googling. I'd been told you could type *anything* into that box. So I hunted and pecked the letters of your name. You were the first thing I googled, my dear.

My darling Mara, famous! How had I been walking around without this knowledge, when perfect strangers might know intimate details of my own daughter's life? Her height, her chest measurements, that she eats an everything bagel with scallion cream cheese for breakfast and always keeps a bottle of prosecco in her fridge. A ballerina. Living in Manhattan, no less! Someone who snacks on post-performance sashimi.

I had to tell someone, anyone. Those heads burrowed in type, in black on white. I cleared my throat to make an announcement. Of course no one would believe me. I see that now. The articles said you were the youngest ballerina ever made a principal dancer. So young, but such presence! The media marvelled. And there I was, a woman in tatters. Face red and raw, greasy hair split-ended. Dirty sweatpants, the only pants I owned, besides my work uniform, that still accommodated my swollen belly. I was well past the age when people might wonder about the belly. Just improperly, overly nourished. I'd been working long shifts at a nursing home, surrounded day in and day out by people slurping the last dregs of life. They often gave me the sweets they were too tired to eat.

In the photos you looked so unattainable, beautiful but scary. Powerful. What a perfect arch to those eyebrows! Something so polished, so haughty, about your beauty. None of the articles mentioned your mother, only your father and stepmother. But I saw myself in the curve of your Achilles tendon, in that bulge of bicep, the concave stomach as your arms lifted over your head. I was young once, too. I once had a body.

The librarian said she would have to ask me to leave if I couldn't be quiet, and so I compromised. I could keep the news to myself, for now, in the interest of research. I used

Google to track your career, starting with the headshots on the ballet company website. You had some competition, I saw, but your photo looked the most natural, your smile the most genuine, your shoulders with the most graceful slope. Why did all the women have naked shoulders in these portraits? Only the male dancers were allowed shirts? And then I found the videos. The computer speakers were disabled, so I only got to know your voice through the closed captioning. I stayed in the library until your image burned my eyes, until the lights dimmed and the throat clearing lacked pretence.

What a life you've had! Clearly the possibility was there, in the genes. I wonder what I could have become, if things had been different.

I'm writing you from the hospital garden, sitting on a white bench in need of repainting, facing away from the brick building so I can pretend I'm somewhere else. I'll have to write in short bursts, because the ragweed makes me sneeze. This place is not fancy enough to employ a gardener, not like the type of place you would surely be sent. Here we must make do with what grows unbidden.

This brings me to my main point, Mara, about what has been growing inside me all these years. I don't want you to worry, but you should be prepared. And so I had to write, to warn you. I see that, now that I'm here. With where you are now, with the resources you surely have at your disposal, there are preventative measures that can be taken. If (god forbid) you end up with this disease, don't let it go so far undetected, like I did. If only I'd known. Years. Black chasms. But, darling, lucidity comes and goes, I must say, and the highs are called highs for a reason. Some call it an illness; others call it a gift.

Mara, it runs through the women in our family like mould through bread. My mother, aunt, grandmother: they all had it, I realize now. It wasn't discussed or, to my knowledge, diagnosed. It was simply accepted that my grandmother was intense, sometimes too much, sometimes hysterical, that she believed her cookbooks contained subliminal messages (if only she could find the right recipe). She disappeared once, when my mother was a child, and it was a week before she was found and hospitalized. Her two daughters took after her. My own mother was a painter who could go days without sleeping, painting all night and tending to me all day. But sometimes she tried to feed me acrylics for breakfast.

I don't want you to go through what I've been through. How much more awful, to have this thing ravage your young, perfect body. It's a disease of the mind, of course, but it has physical consequences, too. Especially if you submit to the drugs. Which I never did. It's the lightest, softest metal, lithium, but so heavy. The least dense of all the solidest elements. Flammable, highly reactive. But the weight gain, the loss of coordination, the hand tremors, the slurring of words that make you sound drunk if your levels become too high. Easy to be mistaken for an alcoholic. To some, that would have been more understandable. I knew all this, which is why I never wanted to take the meds. I was a doctor! I should have been able to handle my moods on my own. Being properly diagnosed would have had disastrous consequences for my professional life. Ironically, though, going undiagnosed is what ended my professional life. So don't listen to me, Mara. Take the goddamn lithium, if it's ever being forced upon you. Some would call my avoidance of it pathological. My psychiatrist here calls it crafty, preferring the language of creativity. I am finally taking it now, at least some of the time. If this letter contains a single coherent thought, that's why. So take note, darling.

At least I was old by the time the illness finally destroyed me. I had periods of remission, periods so long I thought I might escape it, that maybe the curse was broken. But, at the same time, I'd always had this sense I was living on borrowed time, at the height of the wave. All waves crash eventually. So when the tide receded, when the doctor here finally said the words that gave shape to what had been happening to me all these years, long years without you, I wasn't surprised. I'd known it was coming for me. I'd felt its ghoulish shadow underlying even my happiest moments.

You have obviously made good choices, Mara. But I want you to know what's possible. How a single day, a single action, can alter the course of your life. Irreparably. And how you might not be in the right state to notice until it's too late. From where I sit now, in this terrible hospital bed with scratchy lime green sheets (it's raining too hard now to sit in the garden), the choices I should have made seem obvious. Surely you can guess which day I'm referring to?

Something was off-kilter that day, that week, that month— that year, even. Your first year. As an ER doctor, back then, I had to decide a patient's fate in a flash. It weighs on you, being at the reins of all that fate. I'd gone back to work when you were nine months old. I didn't have a choice. Of course I'd rather have stayed with you, but your father lost his job. He wasn't crazy about the idea of staying home, or of me going back to work, but someone had to make money, so I insisted. Doctors are always in demand, I told him, I'll find something quick.

And I did. They talk about compassion fatigue when you're a doctor, but what I felt was pure fatigue. Three months in, my mind often felt untethered from my body, which kept going without me.

After weeks of being alone on break, I finally joined the smokers outside. One day I had a deathly thin agoraphobic patient who hadn't removed her socks or walked in two years. I peeled her socks away for the x-ray, and what little was left of her feet crumpled into my hands like ash. On break, I accepted my first cigarette. After "borrowing" too many cigarettes, I finally bought my first pack.

I'm not telling you all this, Mara, to excuse my behaviour. You're older now, and maybe you'll understand the strange forces that can take hold of a person, the ways we can be ourselves but not ourselves. We are all imperfect beings, after all, hurtling toward our ultimate demise. Some of us are just hurtling faster than others.

You've surely had to make sacrifices to get where you are. Are you your truest self when you're on stage? Or is it when you're alone in your dressing room, after you've taken off your costume and wiped away your makeup? Do you have circles under your eyes without the concealer, after the hours of training? I hope they're not pushing you too hard, but of course they must be.

Do you have someone in your life? Maybe you're the kind who doesn't have time for all that, who has a trainer, nutritionist, hair stylist, makeup artist, publicist, but no one to bring you a glass of that prosecco and give you a foot massage at night. No one to cover you with a blanket when you fall asleep in front of the TV. I know you went through a depression, a period when

Krispy Kreme regularly delivered two dozen glazed donuts to your apartment. I was terrified when I read that, Mara. You got that from me, of course, the binging impulse. One small expression of the depression.

I still think about your YouTube video, that ad campaign with so many views. Your muscles that gleam and ripple. You know, I once had muscles too, my arms sculpted and shaped from years on the school volleyball team. Our coach used to make us do sprints around the track, and after a while I could keep up without having to breath into a brown paper bag. If it hadn't been for a torn ligament during tournament season in senior year, maybe I would have gone somewhere with it.

The clouds outside look threatening, so low and fluffy in the sky that I almost think I could snag one with my finger. Darkening quickly, but for the moment they're still up inside themselves. The afternoon nurse says it's abnormal, how much time I spend watching the clouds. She wonders if I should have been a meteorologist. She has no idea that during my most manic phases, I flew up in and through the clouds, saw them from the inside out. Of course I know she's just making light conversation, that she doesn't really know what's going on in my mind, whether I have an aptitude for science. I've never told her I used to be a doctor myself, that I know the art of patient diversion. I'm not looking to study the science behind rain or lightning. I'm no longer interested in causality. I just like clouds because you can project whatever you want on to them, see what you want to see.

On your first birthday, Mara, I eyed the clock like a sprinter, muscles ready for the gun. I wasn't going to fuck up. Everything was ready, and I was at the top of my game that day, fully prepared and then some. Five-thirty, with the cake. I'd promised your father. I'd traded in a favour for a day shift that ended at 5 P.M.

So I was ready. But at exactly 4:53, as timely as if she'd been sent by a higher power, a shrieking woman staggered through the doors of the ER, her forearm impaled by a fondue skewer with a heart-shaped tip and the white peasant shirt around it a deep, dangerous red. When the paramedic moved out of the way I saw the bigger problem: what looked like the top end of a fence post was protruding from her stomach. She wore gold hoop earrings so large I could have stuck my fist through them. She'd been trying to move objects with her mind, she said. I stared at the daisy-shaped buttons on her sleeveless shirt and wondered about the type of person who has time and energy to waste on such things. Her ID said her name was Abigail but she asked us to call her Lucy.

"Jumped out the window like she was gonna sprout wings," the paramedic muttered to me.

You must understand, Mara, that while yes, the turmoil churning my heart was enough to upset a large vessel in those days, on that particular day, the only thing on my mind was getting home for your birthday. The only thing! You of course weren't old enough to realize the significance of the day, but all I wanted was to be there to see a single striped candle reflected in your eyes, to show you how it's done so you could blow out your own candles as they were added to the cake, year after year. To tug your curly little black pigtails and kiss your silken cheek.

It hadn't been easy. It started during pregnancy, that black cloud that drilled its tentacles into my temples until I could no longer think straight. I guess that kind of thing would more likely be diagnosed now, but back then people didn't think about it so much. If you weren't feeling that glow, something was wrong with you, and you'd sure as hell better hide it. So I did. First I had to stop walking across the bridge to get home after my shift, then riding the subway became dangerous, then driving, and finally even climbing stairs. Once the hospital decided it was too risky for me to keep working, I didn't leave the house, didn't even leave the first floor. I slept in the living room, much to your father's exasperation.

I thought it would get better once you were outside of me, but then, of course, I had even less control. All the things that could harm you, all the ways I could fuck up! I couldn't get you to breastfeed: you rejected me, time after time, until finally I gave up and stuck with the bottle. It felt like such a failure. I was a doctor, after all! I'd never spent much time in the maternity ward, but I'd done a rotation there in school. I knew enough to teach mothers how to breastfeed. I'd heard about the baby blues, but at the time it didn't occur to me that this might have anything to do with me.

So this time, I wasn't going to fuck up. I was going to be a good mother, the one who arrives home on time, with a cake. I paged the doctor taking over my shift, knowing I couldn't leave until this woman was stabilized. I didn't want to say why I had to go; it was hard enough being a female doctor in those days, never mind one with a baby. I worked extra fast, getting the woman bandaged up. The other doctor arrived and I gave my report. The look Abigail/Lucy gave me when I said goodbye, like she knew something I didn't, stopped me cold for a few seconds.

"Don't leave," she said.

I stared at her. But then I shook myself and remembered my purpose.

After a shift I had a hard time transitioning back into the real world. I often felt light-headed, my eyes not quite focusing like they should. Like I'd had a few glasses of wine, though in those days I rarely drank because I knew where it could lead. But that day was different: my focus zeroed in, narrowing to a pinprick. Everything surrounding my focal point was blurry, but I could see everything I needed to see. Giddy with anticipation, I ran to the car, threw open the door, and hurled myself inside.

I'd barely slept in days. After working nights, I tried to spend every minute of my day with you, and something about motherhood reduced my need for sleep. I did my best to keep you happy, Mara, to make up for being away at night. I often took you to the mall down the street, bought you more and more toys, ensuring we had each major shade of the rainbow, until I was running out of room, until they were piling up before I had a chance to take off the tags, until my credit card stopped working and I had to borrow your father's.

At 5:15, I was in the car, revving the engine. Normally it would take twenty minutes to get home. I gave myself a challenge: make it in ten. I was superhuman that day, so I knew I could do it. First, though, I had to pick up the cake. I peeled out of the hospital parking lot and took off toward the bakery, weaving my way through traffic, wondering why on earth everyone was driving so slowly.

I didn't see the 'Closed' sign in the window until I was standing in front of it. I must admit, Mara dear, that I swore. Loudly, too, I'm sure. I stared at the sign, its block lettering

44

that left no ambiguities, unleashing a stream of expletives I won't repeat here. I banged on the door, hopping from foot to foot. Nothing. Not that it matters, the money, but I had paid a lot of it for this cake. An obscene amount. The baker and I had designed it together—this was no cookie-cutter cake, my dear. I couldn't face the thought of going home empty-handed, of seeing my failure in your father's eyes. I panicked, my whole body in a tremble, my eyes stinging. I raised my arms to the sky and pounded them into my thighs in frustration. When I closed my eyes I saw red shapes zinging around so quickly it made my head spin.

A shout from across the street. She was in the doorway of a café, hands wrapped around a huge potted mug. I didn't recognize her at first, without her white hat. Her hair was a bright, rich red, obviously dyed, her face pale like flour. She held up a finger for me to wait and emerged from the café with her coat thrown on unbuttoned. She must have taken pity on me. I was so thrilled I threw my arms around her, telling her all about my shift at the hospital and the gorgeous little daughter waiting for this cake at home.

"It's her first birthday!" I shouted. "My daughter, I mean!"

"I know," said the baker, giving me an odd look.

She opened the shop and handed me the cake. I gave her my best smooch on the cheek and pressed a fifty-dollar bill into her palm. She didn't want to accept, but I insisted, blowing her an air kiss as I ran back to the car.

I set the gold box in the passenger seat and peeked inside, a smile of satisfaction bubbling up inside me until my eyes watered. You should have seen this cake, Mara. A three-tiered pastel dream. So beautiful, so perfect, it made me cry. Your name spelled out on a banner, a bunny holding a balloon with the number 1, and the most exquisite icing flowers lining the edge of each layer. More elaborate than my wedding cake. This cake would make up for the times I hadn't been there to read you *Goodnight Moon*, the times your father had put you to bed storyless.

By then, you slept through the night. The days when your cries reached into my sleep and clutched at my throat with slender fingers until I surrendered into wakefulness were long gone, but I still felt their icy grip. I couldn't get away from the darkness I was so close to falling into, the one I'd thought I could escape by going back to work. Even the ER was better than that darkness, than the constant thread of worries. Slipping down the hardwood stairs, submerging under the bathwater, facing the headlights of an oncoming subway train, launching over the railing separating pavement from river. All with you in my arms. My lack of seniority meant a lot of overnight shifts in the ER, but I was willing. We needed the money, of course, not that your father wanted to admit it, but I suppose in some sense it was also a relief. I knew you were safer with your father.

I drove fast but kept one hand on the box, worried about it sliding and the icing smearing, meanwhile dodging obstacles with the growing suspicion I was being chased. My thoughts raced in front of me and it was hard to keep up. I was the only one with the expertise to save Abigail/Lucy, and I'd left her all alone. A horrible thought. Had your father remembered to clean the powder room? My lipstick probably needed a fresh coat. I checked the mirror and reapplied as I sped through an intersection. I tracked the streetlights, drawing lines with my eyes from one to the next, attracted by the bright lights.

One of them morphed into something colourful and large and sparkling, pleasing, but then it twisted and turned until it became ugly and horrifying, too many shades of red. A large black shape darted across the road, just beyond the periphery of my vision, but when I turned my head, it was gone.

I was having one of my moments, the doctor in me confessed. But the mother in me didn't want to hear it. The road. Concentrate, I told myself. 5:25. I'd lost my own challenge. Shit! Now I was really cutting it close. If I didn't hit any red lights I might arrive almost on time. If I concentrated hard enough, I could turn all the lights green with my mind. I just had to maintain focus.

I didn't want to lose any unnecessary points in the game your father and I played to see who could be the better parent, the better spouse. The game he'd been winning by a landslide, at least in his mind. Your father thought staying home with you automatically made him father of the year. Never mind his lack of job prospects. Once I got home he shut down, slumped in front of the TV beside a growing pile of beer caps. I was a good mother! But we were always understaffed at the hospital and I was perpetually behind on my paperwork. Everything an emergency. It was so hard to balance motherhood and a career in those days, Mara!

Exhaustion often crept up and hit me over the head. Sometimes even while I was driving. That night, though, there wasn't a single detail that escaped my attention. Every molecule came into sharp focus, into slow motion, into …why was everything moving so slowly? How could I drive slow enough to match the pace of this world? Micro movements. Molecules, atoms, subatomic particles. So much dust in the air, it was incredible.

47

I looked down at my hands. They were made up of molecules upon molecules of dust too. So much dirt! How could I use them to protect your cake, darling? I took my hands off the steering wheel, which must have been the source of all that dirt. I pressed my foot down on the accelerator. Who needed hands to drive, really? Your cake needed me more. I had to ensure it was pristine when you blew out that little candle. I could steer with my knees. "Escapade" was playing on the radio, especially for me. I turned up the volume. The universe had begun sending me messages, telling me I was on the right course to making my family whole again.

That's when I saw him. It was his stance that caught my attention, the way he was leaning back with one hand to his chin, eyes raised, like he was deep in thought. He was standing under a streetlight, snow falling around him. Haloed. Maybe he'd been waiting for a bus. He had chin-length hair parted in the middle. A couple days of stubble.

I didn't see the red brake lights until they were too close, already colliding with the front of the car. The ensuing bang resonated through my entire body, from the bones in each toe up through my skull. Is this what the universe was trying to tell me, when it said to *get away* and *save my troubles for another day*? The energy of that impact was like a revelation, orgasm, and disaster all rolled into one. It burned up my legs, through my nether regions, up my torso to the tips of my breasts, and finally through my shoulders and out my head. The sudden silence that followed was stunning. The steering wheel cool against my hot forehead. I felt the panic rise up inside me. In exchange for that fleeting second of ecstasy, I'd fucked up again. I just couldn't seem to stop.

I knew, sometimes at least, that you and your father were in danger with me around. I knew, on some level, that the only way to save you was to disappear. I thought of all the times you wouldn't stop crying but quieted as soon as I put you into your father's arms. He'd give me that pitying look and tell me to go take a nap. The two of you would be fine on your own. You smiled up at him with those big brown eyes.

Knocking on the window.

I looked up, cake smeared across my face, my clothes, the dashboard. We'd locked eyes just before the crash. The stranger opened my door. Janet Jackson was still singing, telling me to leave my worries behind, until I finally turned the key, eyes on the stranger. Silence filled the car, spilling out onto the sidewalk where he was standing.

You won't remember, of course, but I'd made you a special breakfast that morning, small, heart-shaped pancakes with banana slices. And maple syrup, your first taste of sugar. You threw each piece to the floor, crying all the while. I couldn't even make a birthday breakfast that pleased you.

It wasn't easy, leaving you behind every day. But I'd be lying, darling, if I didn't admit that it was also a huge relief. I'd lock myself in the car and go out into the world with only myself to worry about. I didn't turn on the radio as I drove, just enjoyed the soft silence. Also, that was safer, because the radio had begun to send messages. It kept telling me to leave you, Mara, to save you. Which was of course upsetting, not a great way to start the workday.

How could I go home to your father, cake and car—your father's car—totalled? I couldn't, darling. I just couldn't. The stranger extended his hand and helped me out of the car. My car wasn't actually totalled, I realized only later, just dented.

Somewhat miraculously, considering how fast I'd been driving. And the other car was fine. The stranger suggested we get a drink to calm my nerves, a soothing hand on my shoulder. His scent was of tobacco and wool sweaters and bourbon, and I felt my whole body flush. In that moment, stepping out of my life like I'd step out of a pair of high-heeled shoes after a long night felt possible. Leaving all the failure behind. What a relief, not to fuck up anymore! And here was this seductive stranger. So convenient. I saw my chance, a chance I couldn't pass up. The universe told me I needed a little escapade, and then everything would be okay.

My body has long become simply a vehicle, one I'm not particularly attached to. I no longer worry about how clothes look on this body, whether men find me attractive. But back then I still cared. Desperately. I wanted men to find me attractive, craved it, that reflection of my appeal in their eyes, the way their pupils bloomed with desire.

Mania is a difficult state to describe, Mara, but I want to try, so you can identify it should the need ever arise. If your thoughts are moving too fast for you, much less anyone else, to keep up, if you no longer need sleep, just when you feel you're thinking more clearly than you ever have in your life, if you're always the last one to want to leave any party, if the facial expressions of those closest to you morph from amusement to concern to horror … you'll know.

I knew what was happening at home, Mara. Your father would take charge, greet guests and gather presents, enlist some other mothers to help, make some disparaging remark about his disorganized wife, the type of remark I was supposed to grin and bear in his presence, because if I called him out it just made everyone uncomfortable. Maybe Eileen, who lived next door, would help him. I'd seen the way she looked at him and knew she'd be more than willing. (I'm sure we can agree, Mara, that your father was a good-looking man.) You never took to Eileen, even as a baby, and I loved you for that. You knew what she was about, even then. She spoke to you in that fake syrupy voice reserved for babies, and you just stared back at her, un-blinking, unmoved. Could she really be the Eileen who, accord-ing to the internet, took your father's last name and became your stepmother?

I don't mean to paint a nasty portrait of your father here, Mara. He was a lovely man, responsible, capable, dedicated. He was devoted to working hard, defined by his jobs, but without them he could turn mean, fill up with resentment. Sometimes I worried there was something missing deep inside him. I never once saw him cry and though his temper did occasionally fly out of control, it was always directed at an inanimate object, not a person. He was quick to regain control, and was otherwise even-keeled. So different from me. My emotional range could engulf his in a single gulp. Staying at home made him kinder to you, but cruel to me. His cutting remarks would build up and set me off, turn me into someone I did not want to be. We'd become poison to each other.

The truth is, Mara, I don't need to be careful about what I say anymore. I'm old and worn, my life spilled, my cards played.

I like to think I did you a service, leaving when I did, even if that wasn't what I intended at the time. Who knows what would have happened, had I stayed? When those dark thoughts overtook me, I was no longer myself. I used to think of it as taking a ride on my black horse. You weren't safe with me, me and my black horse who would have carted you away.

I used to regret that I didn't breastfeed. I always wondered if I missed out, if that was my original failure. Would we have had a closer bond if I'd been able to feed you from my own breast? But I liked to think the formula provided a more sure supply of nutrients, that you'd grow big and strong. It seems I was right.

I would like to have been the type of mother who took you for a French manicure and to lunch at a café with white table-cloths and carafes of the lightest white wine. We'd eat our salads delicately, using both fork and knife like proper ladies. We'd sip our wine but of course never approach drunkenness.

I was never going to be that mother, Mara. I've never been able to stop at a single glass of wine, and I've always hated the taste of grapefruit.

I can pretend this letter writing is for purely altruistic reasons but of course there's a certain selfishness to it too, a comfort in being known. It brings me pleasure to know I birthed such a being, someone so magnificent, all sinewy muscle. It's only human to want to lay claim to our accomplishments!

I would love to see you command a whole theatre with your presence. You'd never know I was there. You might see the flash of my eyes in a dark sea of audience, but you wouldn't know we share genes.

I did try, Mara. I didn't know if I should tell you, because I didn't want you to feel bad. But after I googled you, before I landed in here, I tried. I took the bus to Manhattan, bought a ticket from a man with green eyes, a scalper, I guess you'd call him. I'd emptied my bank account earlier that day at an ATM in Times Square. What a price you command these days, darling! It's almost obscene. I handed this man the bills in exchange for a neat little rectangle of paper. He had surprisingly well-groomed hands.

Approaching that theatre, the opera house, where it sat glowing in the dark like a forbidden jewel, I was giddy. Absolutely on top of the fucking world. Just look at what I'd done, where I was! There was my last name (my married name, which I've since given up, but still) up on the marquee! I flashed my ticket and entered the building in a daze. Oh, I knew I wasn't properly attired for the occasion, but I thought money got you past that kind of thing.

But I'd just sat down when two guards approached me, said I couldn't stay. I didn't understand. Surely you, darling, wouldn't have wanted that, if you'd known who I was. Surely you didn't know those men in black suits and sunglasses who grabbed my arms and walked me out of the building. Surely you would have scorned those people staring at me, their accusing eyes. Surely, if you'd known, things would have been different. Maybe I wouldn't be here, with these terrible sheets. Maybe I'd be free to leave.

I've only told you one side of my story, Mara. One of my multiple truths.

You've got to believe me, Mara, that I never for a second thought it would be permanent. I needed a break, a night. My *carpe diem* moment, running off with a stranger. I just needed a small swath of time where I didn't feel like a failure. It's called mania for a reason. I didn't know what I was doing!

Carpe diem is a cliché best left to movies about dead poets.

Your father, he's a man who stands by his beliefs. Joint custody would be a given, I thought at first. Not so. He made sure of that.

When I got out of the stranger's bed the next morning, your first day as a one-year-old, there were two smudges on the pillowcase where my eyes had been. While he was in the shower, I flipped the pillow over and slipped out.

I went back to the car and got in to think. The icing had hardened on the dash, covering the air vents. I turned on the heat and the fragrance of sickly sweet sugar filled the car. I leaned back, closed my eyes. It smelled like the lilac perfume my grandmother always wore.

Sometimes I think about Abigail/Lucy, the woman with the unnaturally large earrings. If she hadn't stabbed herself, if she'd come in five minutes later, what would have happened? What if the red-haired baker hadn't materialized from the café? Would I have missed the stranger? Would the rest of my life, our lives, have turned out differently? Would you still be who you are, Mara?

Later that day, I drove to the house, our house, and was shocked to see it unchanged. Smoke billowing from the chimney into the chilly day, curtains drawn. It didn't look upset at all. I knew you and your father were safe there, snuggled in together. I knew he would feed you Cheerios with the patience to make sure each bite made it into your mouth. He was so much better at the airplane games.

I left the gold box containing a rebaked, reconstructed cake on the front steps for you.

I don't expect you to ever forgive me, Mara, but I had to drive away.

Rabbits with Red Eyes

My Uncle Tony was diagnosed with lung cancer when he was forty-five. That same day, he pulled on his hip waders, grabbed his shotgun, and plunged into the Sevogle. It was late fall, the water ice cold, and the crimson leaves of the river-banked birch trees were spiralling to their deaths on either side of him. He kept his eyes skyward, already imagining his sweet surrender, and held the gun over his head as his waders filled with water. After the shot rang out, he slipped under the surface until he was carried away by the current.

At least that's how I imagined it when I finally found out what happened, much later. My father said Tony didn't want to live like that, once he knew what was spreading inside him. He didn't even wait to find out whether it was treatable. His body washed up to shore not far from the cabin that had been his home for the past twenty-five years. He'd tossed his fishing line into that river hundreds of thousands of times, casting his hopes on trout, the brown kind with red spots. When trout swim out to sea their skin turns silver, but back in the river the glistening silver sheds to reveal a dull brown. The thought that even fish face faded glory made me sad.

I only met Uncle Tony once, less than a year before he died. I had just turned twelve, and it was an unseasonably humid spring day. My parents had taken my brother and me on a day trip to Mactaquac, a provincial park, but our beach time had been cut short by a sudden downpour. We spread muddy beach towels over the seats for the drive home, the car smelling up like swamp. My father drove fast, my mother beside him taking furtive sips from a can of Moosehead that had been half full when the rain started, and my brother and me in back counting the seconds between the lightning and the thunder. The storm was gaining on us.

When we pulled into our driveway, Tony was leaning against a burnt-orange pickup truck wearing bright yellow boots and a green rain jacket with the hood up, his grey face long and drawn.

"Who's that?" I asked.

"That's your Uncle Tony," my father said.

His voice sounded strangely flat.

"Really? How's he related to us?" asked my brother.

"He's my brother," said my father.

This was news to my brother and me. Silence filled the car as we all gazed at my father's brother through the rainy windshield. He was looking over us at the sky.

My mother slipped her hand into the space between the headrest and my father's neck. She gently massaged the soft spot she found there, making small circles with her fingers. She only did that when he was upset, and it seemed to calm him down. It only worked for her, though. I tried it once and my father batted me away, laughing, as if I was one of those pretty but ultimately annoying fluorescent blue dragonflies that come out in June.

"Stay here," my father said.

He got out of the car and spoke to Tony, who kept motioning toward the backyard with a wide sweep of his arm so emphatic I worried it was going to fly out of its socket. Tony's hood fell to reveal crusty blond curls, hollow cheeks, a red nose, grey circles beneath wild eyes. I watched his arm go back and forth five times (I counted) before I jumped out of the car and ran past my father's outstretched fingers into the backyard.

I found two white rabbits with red eyes. Their fur matted from the rain, they cowered in the corner of a crude cage constructed of chicken wire and plywood. They whimpered as I approached. The cage had no top, and none of the nails had been hammered all the way in.

I never saw Uncle Tony again after his truck sped out of our driveway that day, but our parents let us keep the rabbits. I named them Tony the First and Tony Two Two.

We moved to a new house on the other side of town not long after, across the river that divided the city. It happened fast, and I didn't understand why we had to move, why I had to leave my friends behind and change schools. My favourite thing about our first house was the tree house my brother and I found out front among a protective circle of neck-achingly tall trees. I wanted to turn the smell into a scratch-and-sniff sticker to take with me: the crunch of pine needles under our feet, the head-clearing scent of fresh pine and earth after it rained.

The new house had no trees or flowers in the yard. Too new for that. But my father built the rabbits a proper cage, one that was closed in, and we filled it with hay to keep them warm. At first he said we couldn't bring the rabbits into the house, but I snuck them in so often he finally gave up.

"Keep them in the sun porch, at least."

My father kept his computer in there, and the rabbits chewed through the power cord. Tony Two Two was the real culprit, I knew, but Tony the First had to share equally in my father's door-slamming wrath. I was afraid for Tony the First and Tony Two Two after that. My father's temper had always been unpredictable. The sun porch was mostly empty after he moved the computer to the basement, so I built obstacle courses and started the rabbits on a training program. I hoped a structured dollop of education would keep them out of trouble.

Helping my mother unpack one afternoon, I came across a box of old photo albums. In an envelope of outtakes, I found a crinkled photo of my father and Uncle Tony. I knew it was them because their names were pencilled on the back: George, age 8, and Anthony, age 11. In the photo Tony is a foot taller and has his arm slung around my father, who's holding up a fish almost half as big as he is. They wear identical sun-slackened grins, two brothers content after an afternoon of fishing. They used to love each other, I thought.

I was in a theatre the night Uncle Tony died. My mother took me to see *Before Sunrise* because she knew how much I liked Ethan Hawke, and I went even though I was too old to go to the movies with my mother. I made sure we arrived late and sat at the back where no one would see us. My fingers got greasy from the buttery popcorn and I drank so much root beer I had to go to the bathroom halfway through the movie. I didn't dry my hands, lamenting those lost four minutes of Ethan time.

When we got home, my father was sitting at the kitchen table drinking a beer in the dark. My mother turned on the light and asked him what was wrong. He blinked in the sudden brightness, his expression more raw than I'd ever seen it.

"The rabbits are gone," he said.

"What?" I demanded.

My father shrugged, his eyes on his hands.

"They must have run away," he said.

I stared at him, but he still wouldn't look at me. Then he told us about Tony. Not the details, just that his brother had "passed on." No one said anything for a few seconds, and then my mother suggested I go find my brother and watch a movie.

"I just saw a movie," I said.

"Your father and I need to talk."

My father looked up. After seeing the expression in his eyes, I never brought up the rabbits again.

My brother was on his stomach in front of the TV, face propped up by small hands. He was two years younger, so breaking the news was my responsibility.

"Uncle Tony died," I said.

"Who?" asked my brother.

"Tony. Dad's brother?"

He looked up at me, confused.

"Don't you remember, when he brought the rabbits?"

"Oh."

He turned his attention back to the TV, where Steve Urkel was on the screen in a rerun of *Family Matters*. When the commercials came on, he sat up and turned to face me.

"Are we supposed to cry?" he asked.

"Um, I guess? I don't know. We didn't really know him."
Neither of us had ever known someone who died before.
"I can't remember his face."
"I can."
"Where's Dad?"
"Talking to Mom."

We both understood that when my mother said she had to talk to my father, we were to make ourselves scarce.

That night, I dreamt about the rabbits. I was in the woods, chasing streaks of white and the glow of red eyes, and I couldn't catch them. Finally I stopped, unable to catch my breath, and when I straightened up I saw them in a small clearing several feet ahead of me. They too had stopped, in front of a man. He had Tony's face, hooded by his green rain jacket. He looked at me and seemed about to speak. I had a hundred questions on the tip of my tongue, and something told me he was ready to answer them. But then I woke up.

My mother was alone in the kitchen when I went downstairs the next morning.

"Morning, honey. How about some breakfast?"
"Where's Dad?" I asked.

My father made breakfast on Saturday mornings. He took pride in his poached eggs. The secret, he said, was to swirl the water into a gentle whirlpool before cracking the eggs. He always scooped two perfect fluffy white mounds onto my plate, and I loved to cut into them right away, watch the shock of yellow ooze out over my mother's fancy white plate and catch it with my toast. My brother got picked up early on Saturdays for hockey practice, and it was the only time I was ever alone with my parents. Sometimes they even let me drink a small cup of coffee with maple syrup. I took a section of my father's paper to read while I sipped.

"He's out," she said. "French toast sound okay?"

My mother's manner was excessively chipper. She looked different. Peering at her, I finally realized she wasn't wearing any makeup. I rarely saw my mother before she'd applied her rouge. She was a watered-down version of herself without it. And until now I'd never noticed that she must colour in her eyebrows every morning, too.

"Out where?"

"He'll be back later," she said.

"Later when?"

"I don't know, honey," she said, strain starting to snake its way through her voice. "Let me make us some breakfast."

While we ate the soggy French toast, which I didn't like nearly as much as my father's eggs, I asked why my father had never told us about Uncle Tony. How could I have gone twelve years without knowing my father had a brother?

"Tony and your father didn't get along," she said.

"Why not?" I asked.

"Well, your father didn't approve of some of his decisions."

"What decisions?"

"We used to have to drive up to his cabin when the neighbours called," she said. "When you kids came along, your father decided enough was enough."

"But what was wrong with him?" I asked.

"Your father never wanted to drag you kids into it," she said.

I could see she already felt like she had said too much.

"Seriously, Mom, you don't need to baby me."

But she had already forgotten about me and was looking out the window, moon-eyed. I sighed loudly, but she continued to ignore me. I followed her gaze. Two chickadees were sitting at the bird feeder, pecking at each other. I couldn't tell whether they were kissing or fighting.

My mother was obsessed with birds. She kept a diary, not of the events of her daily life, but of the birds she saw each day and their movements, their calls. She could have spent an entire day with binoculars ringing her eyes, charting birds through the picture window. Her unusually large blue eyes seemed especially suited to this. She even looked a little like a bird, with her long, pointy nose. To me, birds were boring.

My father didn't come back until late that evening. I was already in bed when I heard the telltale clank of the garage door being locked. That was the first of many such disappearances in the weeks to follow. My mother wouldn't tell me where he was. He was dealing with things and I should leave him be, she said. When he returned, he was always quieter than normal, more contemplative, calmer. He no longer noticed when I left my dishes on the counter instead of putting them in the dishwasher, his temper less likely to flare out of control. I tiptoed around, afraid to make too much noise around him.

I went into the kitchen one night and was startled to see him sitting there looking through a photo album. I hadn't heard him come home.

"Some of the pictures are falling out," he said, holding up a Polaroid. "I guess the glue only holds so long."

I watched as he paged through the album.

"I wish you'd had the chance to meet Tony when he was younger," he said. "He was brilliant back then. We had a lot of fun."

I sat down at the table, hoping he'd say more, but he shut the album.

"Time for you to get to bed, missy," he said.

My father came home one day in an orange pickup truck laden with boxes. He'd cleaned out Tony's cabin. His parents long dead, my father was the only person left to do it. He carted the boxes down to a corner of the basement and threw an old blanket over them. The next time he disappeared, I snuck downstairs when my mother was busy ironing. I opened the boxes one by one in a guilty panic, hurrying in case I was discovered. I was surprised by what I found. A diploma from McGill University declaring that Anthony Stonehill was a Doctor of Philosophy in Physics, sheet music for Chopin's "Scherzo No. 2" and Brahms' "Rhapsody in B Minor," a collection of faded baseball cards from the '70s. A framed photo of a younger Uncle Tony and a blonde woman I didn't recognize. His wife? I was delving into a box of old records when I heard footsteps behind me. I'd been so engrossed that I hadn't heard my father come home.

"Put that away," he said quietly, before going back upstairs without another word.

I returned to the basement the next chance I got, but the boxes were gone. Through the basement window I saw the rabbit cage, empty.

Early one Saturday morning, my father came into my room and asked if I wanted to come with him.

"Come where?"

"Fishing."

I had never fished. We stopped at Canadian Tire and my

father bought me a child-sized rod. I was small for my age and I wasn't very strong. I was pleased that my father had chosen me for this voyage and not my brother.

"It's just for learning," he said. "We can get you a bigger one later."

We rolled through the Tim Horton's drive-through. My father let me get a coffee even though my mother always said I was too young to get started on a Tim's habit. I ordered a double double, two creams and two sugars. I rolled up the rim when I was finished, but I didn't win. I held the cup out the window, feeling the pressure of the wind against my hand, and when my father wasn't looking I let go, turning to watch the cup fly away into the distance until it was a tiny brown speck.

When we got to the river an hour out of town, I did cart-wheels all the way from the car to the riverbank. I would have to sit absolutely still to avoid scaring the fish, my father told me as he hooked a worm on the end of my rod.

"Gross," I said.

I sunk the worm into the river. Nothing happened for a long time, and then something did. I felt a little tug.

"Hey!" I yelped.

"Shhh … keep steady," said my father.

He helped me reel it in and we let the fish fall to the ground. Small, it flopped around on the rocks, back and forth, its gills gulping for air and mouth speaking soundlessly. It had red spots all over its back, a pretty orange stripe along each side of its body. Its gills spasmed and seized the way my leg did when I got a charley horse. I could see its red guts underneath flexed gills.

Its impending death hit my stomach in a rush like it had a physical form, something pointy and hard, and I couldn't breathe. I turned away from my father, thinking I might be sick.

"We can throw it back," my father said. "It's too small, anyway."

I guess he saw it in my face. He unhooked the fish and tossed it gently back into the water. It didn't move at first, but then it slowly swam away. I was embarrassed and relieved.

On the way back to the car, we passed a cabin with purple curtains in the windows.

"That's where Tony lived," my father said. "He loved this river."

We stood there for a few minutes without saying anything.

"I'm sorry about your rabbits," my father finally said.

"That's okay," I said, because I didn't yet know how to tell him it wasn't.

Fulminology

We're sock-footed around the kitchen island, clutching goblets of white wine and chipping away at the cheese my mother has set out on a wooden cutting board. Alex is at the stove, batting at onions in a frying pan with one hand and waving the other to punctuate his story about why you don't want to get into an elevator with Steve Jobs. I keep one ear on the conversation and let the other roam inward. Rain is pounding a staccato on the windows, and lightning flashes as Alex's story reaches its climax. I'm the only one who notices the lightning, its impeccable timing.

"You don't become the CEO of Apple by being a nice guy," says Alex, his tone admiring.

Alex is a shortcut through the debilitating self-consciousness that runs in my family and slows us down. He moves quickly, confidently, pausing only to toss a wave of brown hair out of his eyes as he orchestrates the meal. My mother can't chop a vegetable without asking how she should slice it. Now she rubs her lower back, waiting for someone to inquire about her sciatica. My father's glasses have slipped down his nose as he peers at his Blackberry, texting his friend to make golf plans. My parents have remodelled since I was last home, and I'm disoriented by the gleam of the fancy range hood and matching gas stove against the familiar butter-yellow walls.

"So, Jessie. How's work, honey?" asks my mother.

"Fine," I say.

Alex and I last saw my parents a year ago, in Cuba, and I've switched jobs twice since then. I didn't want to come. I give myself one day every year. This day. A day when wallowing is permitted and even encouraged. A day of pyjamas, a bottle of Merlot, a bar of dark chocolate, a box of Kleenex. A day to watch one of my brother's favourite movies, *The Blair Witch Project* or *The Evil Dead*, inappropriate though they are for the occasion.

But my mother had insisted. She'd called and talked to Alex.

"Wine?" she asks now, hovering the Pinot Grigio over the glass in front of me.

Her glass is empty, and she wants my permission to fill both. I hesitate. But I don't want to give my parents the wrong idea, an answer to the unasked question that hung over the dinner table in Cuba. The hope that would ripple across my mother's face. *Is she?*, she'd ask my father later, while loading the dishwasher. Alex wouldn't want that; he squirms any time I insinuate we've been trying. *We haven't really been trying,* he keeps telling me. *My swimmers are strong*: his mantra. But it's been two years since we decided to stop not trying and I went off the pill.

"What happens, happens," he'd said.

His favourite expression. Hard to argue with its finality, and a gleeful smirk crosses his face each time he has the chance to use it.

67

My mother is still looking at me, tilting her head like the inquisitive chickadees that grace her bird feeder. Earlier, I'd noticed the avalanche threat posed by a small mountain of wine bottles in the recycling bin.

"Sure," I say.

She pours.

Drink till it's pink. I am strangely comforted by the asinine motto found on fertility message boards, and I ignore its angelic twin, *sober till it's over.* In any case, it's too soon. It's been less than a month since the last pregnancy test, the single pink line on the bathroom floor, that fake marble pattern, shiny white with swirls of grey. The pee-stained line appeared almost immediately, but I waited, watching it from my perch on the toilet. The pink line stayed constant, mocking me with its pretence at cheeriness.

I use pregnancy tests the way some people preemptively pop ibuprofen. A pregnancy test can change your life in a flash. At some point, I began to resent its finality. Once I see the single pink line, the possibility is pushed back down beneath the surface, and the waiting begins again. A hope and a threat. I've never been regular, my body denying me the natural barometer that most women take for granted. Each time I get a negative result, I am that much closer to wanting a positive result. Piled together, all the plastic pregnancy tests with their single pink lines would fill a small waste bin by now.

"You're not pregnant," Alex has told me many times, usually while handing me a glass of wine.

The utter certainty in his voice always surprises me. Despite his lack of logic, I believe him. His confidence is contagious. Alex knows things, practical, life-living things. He can dissolve my fears with a dismissive kiss. A pointed look can stop me cold, mid-obsession. Everything felt so uncertain for so long. After I met Alex, I could finally stand with two feet on the ground.

But what if he's wrong? So I do the tests anyway, more often than is practical. I hide the evidence so he won't complain about the expense.

My glass of wine disappears faster than I intend.

"So," Alex says. "Are you finished with the renovations?"

"Only the kitchen," says my father. "We haven't touched the upstairs."

"I'm thinking I might make one of the bedrooms into a meditation room," says my mother.

My father and I look at her.

"Meditation?" asks my father.

"I've been taking classes at the Y," she says.

"When?"

"Not all of us spend our lives on the golf course," she says. "And not all of us have buddies with the leisure time to tee off every morning."

"Where else do I have to be?"

"It's important to keep the mind active. At my age, it could betray me any day now."

"Which room?" I ask.

"The middle one," my mother says. "Not your old room, the other one."

A familiar lump in my throat. I swallow hard.

The lightning flashes again. This time it fills the kitchen and everyone notices. The thunder is so loud the dishes rattle, and then the lights go out.

Lightning has always fascinated me. How it comes out of no-where, splits through the sky preceding its lumbering companion, the thunderous bang. My brother Dean used to call me the lightning whisperer, because I could sense it coming with startling accuracy. The same way I always knew what time it was without wearing a watch.

"Maybe you should become a fulminologist," Dean said once.

"A what?" I asked.

"Fulminology, the study of lightning. C'mon, Jess. Weren't you listening in science class?"

I was never one for science. Not like Dean. My brother possessed none of my arcane gifts, but he had other talents. More practical, parent-appreciable things, like scoring the winning goal, wordlessly shovelling the driveway or raking leaves. His real passion was film—he carried his camcorder everywhere—but our parents thought his future lay in the rational comforts offered by the sciences.

My parents: sports-team-cheering, meat-and-potatoes types. They didn't know what to do with me. My fascination with lightning, levitation, poltergeists, chakras, tarot cards, paganism, and Arthurian legends didn't give them much to cheer about. One summer they put me in a girls' softball league. I missed any ball that came my way, usually because I'd been thinking up a plot twist for the fan-fiction that filled several Hilroys stuffed under my mattress. I preferred to stay home with my books and burn my favourite incense, which the guy at the occult shop down-town said was specially crafted to inspire creativity.

Then there was Dean and his underground horror films, his fake blood recipes and basement séances. But Dean was better at creating a veneer for our parents. They thought he actually liked hockey.

My mother gets out the candles and we move to the table to eat sunflower-yellow butternut squash soup, into which Alex folded the caramelized onions and a trail of nutmeg. The table, at least, hasn't changed. Cheap cherrywood, with a big nick from when Dean almost chopped his finger off carving a pumpkin. The candlelight gives the room a Halloween-ish glow, everyone's faces flickering.

My father raises his eyebrows when I put a bowl in front of him. He glances at Alex, who's still busy at the stove.

"Does he always do the cooking?"

I shrug.

"I cook, too. Well, sometimes."

"If by cook, you mean that she has our favourite sushi take-out place on speed dial," Alex says as he brings the other bowls to the table.

"I had sushi once, when I lived in Montreal in the late '70s. My boss threw a party, thought he was being avant-garde. We all got food poisoning and had to call in sick the next morning. No one left to answer the phones," my mother says.

It's been years since I've sat at this table. My parents are in the seats they've always taken. I'm in Dean's old seat, and Alex is in mine. I'm feeling nauseous.

I close my eyes, willing someone to break the slurpy silence, which is almost as bad as popcorn crunching during a quiet moment in a movie theatre. A crack of thunder brings relief to the tension in my shoulders.

"You know," says my mother, her face shadowed, "I read an

article about nutmeg in the *Times* the other day. Apparently it can cause miscarriages."

She takes a large gulp of her wine, eyes wide, waiting. I cough on a spoonful of soup.

"*Now*, Mary," says my father. This is a running joke in my family, an imitation of my grandfather's way of dismissing things out of hand.

"They used it to end pregnancies in the Middle Ages," she continues.

"I'm sure you'd need a lot more than what I put in the soup," says Alex, patting me on the back.

I swallow.

"They should put a warning on these things. My friend Melanie's daughter was told by her doctor not to drink *herbal tea* during her pregnancy," she says. "Who would have thought?"

"Hey, we haven't even told you about our trip to Italy yet," says Alex.

He refills my mother's wine glass as I watch the bottle, willing it to right itself.

When I was ten, I became convinced I could move things just by looking at them. I stared at the ceramic angel on my night table, practicing, willing it to rise from its perch. Had I done any research, I would have learned that I should have started with something lighter, easier. Like making a pencil roll across the table. The angel stayed firmly planted on the night table, its wings useless. I was a telekinetic failure. For a while I campaigned for a poltergeist to haunt our house, but that ended when Dean made me watch *Poltergeist* one night. I slouched around for days after that, zombie-eyed from terrified lack of sleep. Dean just laughed, jumping out from corners and throwing objects to startle me.

Dean was two years older, but only one year ahead in school. He'd had to repeat a grade early on, something I was forbidden from ever bringing up. His friends came over after school and they'd hole up in the basement with their horror flicks. I used to watch with them, but around the time I started high school something changed.

I hovered at the top of the stairs, listening, intuiting that I was no longer welcome.

"Where's your sister?" Dean's friend Josh asked one day.

"Who, that fat cow? Why do you care?"

I stomped up to my room as loudly as I could. I'd show him fat cow.

I kept to my room when Dean's friends were over after that. When they weren't around, though, things were different. Dean and I communicated through games. Sunday mornings, board games, blueberry Eggo waffles. He always won. We didn't talk to talk, but with a board game in front of us, it was easier to let conversation float to the surface. When Dean had that look of concentration, when I was so intently engaged without being scrutinized, I felt at peace.

"I couldn't sleep last night," Dean told me one Sunday.

He was rubbing his eyes. Our parents had gone to church, and I'd been concentrating on my next Monopoly move, trying to figure out how I was going to buy Park Place.

Dean always had nightmares, and I was used to an occasional shout penetrating my sleep. It wasn't something we talked about. But that day he told me about a dream that had been recurring for five years, the unbearable headaches that followed.

73

A pair of red eyes chasing him through impenetrable darkness, until he came upon a skeleton sitting under a tree in the woods behind our house. Fear bloomed in his eyes as he described it.

"This last time, it was wearing my scarf," he said.

I shudder.

"It gets so loud in my head after I wake up, I have to drown it out with something else," he continues. "Loud music."

"You play loud music in the middle of the night?"

"I use headphones, moron."

After that, whenever I woke up in the middle of the night, I wondered if Dean had his headphones on in the next room. If I knocked on the wall, would he hear me?

Alex brushes at his upper lip with his hand. I stare at him, then realize he's trying to tell me to wipe my face. I dutifully use my napkin.

"Better?" I ask.

He nods. He always makes me feel like a child when I have something on my face.

We're eating steak, juicy blood flowing with each cut of the knife, and Alex fills our glasses from a decanter he's been hiding in the kitchen. The wine is the same colour as the blood on our plates. My head is starting to spin, just enough so my words leave me before I can catch them and rein them in.

"It's weird to be home," I say, gazing at the apple-shaped clock Dean made in high school shop class.

My father is shuffling his meat around on his plate. He likes his steak well done. The blood, I know, is too much for him. I should have told Alex.

"We're so glad you guys could make it this weekend," says my mother. "We see you so little."

She says this carefully, like she does most things, her sentences bubbling with the hot stew of resentment that's been simmering inside her for years. Since I moved away, my parents have come to visit exactly once. After Alex came into the picture, we convinced them to meet us somewhere warm, Florida and then Cuba. Neutral ground.

"It was about time I saw the place where Jess grew up," says Alex.

"I thought we should all be together," says my mother. "For this."

She won't say his name. A small ball of anger grows in my chest, fed by the wine.

"And travelling may not always be so easy," she says. "Like if you were ever to have a child."

I look up just in time for a large flash of lightning that obliterates the expression on my face.

He tried to tell me.

After I went away to university, Dean moved into my old room. It was bigger, with more light. With an extra room between him and my parents, maybe he didn't need to wear headphones in the middle of the night anymore. Dean hadn't gone to university. Instead, he worked at the movie theatre and created his own syllabus, a stack of DVDs. Our parents told people he was taking a year off, but one became two. When I came home at Christmas, he said he'd been counting the glow-in-the-dark stars I'd left on the ceiling when he couldn't sleep.

A high school friend was having a party at his family's cabin in the woods that night. Dean kept going on about *The Blair Witch Project*, incredulous that I hadn't seen it yet.

"Unlike you, I've been busy studying," I said.

"You have to see this movie, Jess," he said. "It's wild. Unlike anything else, even *The Evil Dead*. Come to the early show before the party. I can sneak you in."

Even though he'd already seen it twice, Dean took a long break to sit beside me. I hid my eyes during the scariest parts, but he kept watching.

When it was over, I didn't move.

"Wait," I said. "Did that really happen?"

He cracked a half smile.

"We'll never know."

I drove out the deserted Mazerolle Settlement Road toward the party, threatening trees lurching with the hangover of the jumpy documentary-style camera lens. Cowering beneath the steering wheel, I hyperventilated and used my father's government-issued car phone to call Dean, who was still at the theatre.

"I think I'm lost."

"Relax," he said, the line crackling. "Keep driving. There's only one way to go. You'll find it eventually."

He was right. I kept going until I saw the glow of a five-foot-high bonfire that meant I'd found the party. My friend appeared out of the shadows to hand me a beer.

My vision was already dancing when Dean showed up an hour later.

"Hey," I said, surprised.

"Just checking," he said. "Make sure you didn't get eaten by a witch."

I passed him a beer, but he put it aside to take out his camcorder. He trained it on me. I frowned at him—I've always hated being caught on film. He turned the camera around and pointed it at himself. I watched him on the small flip screen.

The bonfire was flickering on his face, the trees lurking behind him. The camera exaggerated the dark circles under his eyes, his skin ghostly white in contrast. A terrible heat surged up my spine, jolting through me.

"C'mon," he said, "into the woods."

He wanted footage, I knew that. I still didn't want to go with him. But when he grabbed my arm and pulled me along, I didn't fight.

We were far away from the others when he took the camera out again and focused it on my face. I was breathing heavily from my attempt to match his pace.

"How do you feel?" he asked.

I heard a branch snap a few feet away.

"Scared," I said.

I could see his finger working the zoom inward.

After a few minutes he turned the camera off and put it in his jacket pocket. He closed his eyes and massaged his temples with his fingers.

He grabbed both my arms so suddenly I jumped. He stared at me as if he wanted me to read his thoughts.

"What?"

"It's been weird, without you in the house," he said.

I didn't like the way he was gripping my arms. I felt trapped by the pain I could read on his face even in the darkness.

"Something's not right," he said. "With me, I mean."

I knew I should ask what was wrong but all I could think about was getting away from him. I wasn't ready to take his confession. I'm not wired for confessions.

"You're hurting me," I said, trying to pull my arms from his grasp.

"Good," he said, gripping them harder.

The animal in his eyes.

I struck without thinking, ran without looking, crashed through trees. I was back at the bonfire, panting, before I knew what happened.

Later, I searched everywhere for the footage from that night, wanting to separate the imaginary from reality. But it had disappeared.

Alex empties the decanter evenly among our four glasses. It's barely perceptible, but my mother is swaying, humming under her breath. My father is staring into space, no longer making any attempt at conversation.

"A meditation room sounds nice," says Alex. "My boss swears by transcendental meditation."

Alex can't stand silence.

"Like David Lynch," I say.

Now there was a filmmaker for Dean. Horror, tragedy, comedy, human emotion and frailty all wrapped into one.

Alex's brown eyes meet mine for a moment. Startled by their naked compassion, I look away.

"Dean thought meditation was for losers," I say.

I try to keep my tone light, but my statement falls on the conversation with the grace of a wet wool blanket. Alex clears his throat. Everyone looks down at their plates. Just then, the lights come back on. We all look at each other in surprise, blinking.

When it happened, I was studying for midterms. All day, a vague dread followed half a step behind me. I moved from my dorm room to the cafeteria and from the cafeteria to the café and finally to the bar, but I couldn't shake it—it kept growing until I was short of breath and tried to lubricate it with a glass of red wine. I had a physics exam the next day, but I couldn't focus.

That night, my parents called me at the dorm. There was only one phone for the whole hall, and the girl next door knocked to say it was for me. The receiver was sitting on top of the radiator, and it was warm when I put it to my ear.

"Jessie," my mother said, "it's Dean."

I took the first flight home.

My parents were at the hospital when I arrived, so I grabbed a taxi at the airport. The driver put the wipers on high speed against the searing rain. I found my parents in the waiting room.

"We can't go in," my mother said.

"What happened?"

"We don't know," said my father.

"But did they find out who hit him?" I asked.

"No," said my father. "They don't think there was another car."

"There was a big storm," said my mother, her voice cracking. "Hail, thunder, lightning, the works."

Dean was found outside city limits, way out the Hanwell Road on Mazerolle Settlement Road. Not far from where my friend's bonfire had been, a passing police officer noticed Dean's car in a ditch. The front bumper was ripped clean off, the bowels of the car exposed. Dean was lying on the grass a few steps away, his empty camcorder on the ground beside him, his arms stretched up and palms pillowing his head, as if he were watching the stars. Except his eyes were closed.

"How is he?" I asked.

My parents looked at each other, and then at me.

"He's not great, Jess," my father said.

My mother put her arm around me, awkward. That's when I knew things were really bad. The thunderous bang brought me to my knees.

Alex reaches a hand toward me.

"I'm sorry," he says softly.

I look down at the blood left on my plate, unable to formulate a proper response. Alex's hand weighs on my shoulder. I'd been attracted by his dogged practicality, a personality trait that had always eluded me, but at moments like this I feel the outer limits of his emotional range.

"How about dessert?" my father asks.

"Sure," says Alex, withdrawing his hand. "Whaddya got?"

"I think there's some ice cream in the freezer."

"Oh, Malcolm, that's been there for ages," my mother says. "It's probably all gummy by now."

I get up and float toward the stairs.

After Dean died, my parents started sleeping in separate rooms. My mother still kept her clothes in their shared bedroom, but she slept in Dean's room, the one that had been mine before I left. I couldn't figure out whether this was her way of staying closer to Dean, or of staying away from my father. She never mentioned the stars.

The big question was too overwhelming, so I became fixated on all the small, simple things I should have asked my brother. *Are you dating anyone? What's your favourite food? Do you read books? What was the happiest moment of your life? The saddest? Where would you live if you could live anywhere?* I started writing the questions down in a tiny blue notebook.

They say lightning doesn't strike twice. But I hadn't sensed the velocity of what was coming, and I felt betrayed, unhinged. I couldn't predict anything anymore. The university needed a copy of the death certificate to excuse me from midterms. That was the last in a list of things that made me want to kick holes in cupboard doors, like Dean had done once during an especially tense fight with our mother.

I never went back to my dorm. Instead, I took the Greyhound to Montreal and found a cheap room in a student neighbourhood. I got a job at a Second Cup on Queen Mary Road where they weren't so worried about my rusty French. Business was slow on the late night shift. I tried to float a spoon with my mind. I swear I saw it move once, just a touch, a preparation for flight. But then a customer cleared her throat, wanting to order her vanilla hazelnut decaf latté, and broke my concentration.

I discovered a talent for churning out lattés with perfect foam density. They moved me to the busy shift, and there was no time for spoon bending. That suited me just fine, because I was trying hard not to think.

Three years later, I was sickened by the hundreds of thousands of lattés I'd foamed since Dean's accident. All the espresso had seeped into my pores. No matter how furiously I scrubbed, I couldn't rid my fingers of the burnt coffee smell. I got on another Greyhound and moved west slowly. I took a ferry to Vancouver Island and rented a small, boxy apartment a short walk from driftwood, seaweed, and the ocean breeze. In Victoria, I was almost as far away from home as I could get without leaving the country entirely. I needed as much physical distance from him as possible. Before I was eaten alive, like in one of his horror films.

I was nodding off on the beach one afternoon, propped up against a piece of driftwood, when a shadow fell over me. I opened my eyes and met Peter. He'd been stood up, and he had an extra americano. He was doing an honours thesis in philosophy, concentrating on Hegel. He tried to explain the Hegelian dialectic, something about a thesis, an antithesis, and a synthesis, arriving at a higher truth. I smiled and nodded, took another sip of my coffee. The best americano I'd ever had, as it turned out. Peter promised to tell me where it came from only if he could take me there himself.

After Peter walked off down the beach, I took out my blue notebook. *Do you drink coffee?* I wrote. *Do you know anything about Hegel?*

Peter shared a place with his friend Nathan, a musician, and it was the messiest apartment I'd ever seen. But in Peter's room, the door closed, everything was okay. Black satin sheets and dim lights, candles and incense for effect. He played Belle and Sebastian on his guitar when it was sunny and Portishead through speakers he'd mounted on the wall when it got dark and he wanted to keep his hands free. We drank cheap red wine and it was the best sex I'd ever had. He was attentive. I funnelled rage into passion.

But then my period didn't come. Stress, I thought. I hadn't yet been inducted into the purchasing of pregnancy tests. The next month, it came with a vengeance. I couldn't keep it at bay, and finally I surrendered to it, climbing into the bathtub and staying there through the waves of pain that punctuated the night. It flowed everywhere, bright red oozing and clotting all over the white ceramic I'd worked so hard to keep clean because otherwise my landlady would charge me a damage deposit when I finished my degree and moved out. It kept flowing and flowing, until it stopped. I hadn't known there was something to lose until it was already lost.

When I climbed out of the bathtub the next morning, it had been exactly five years since Dean's death. The significance wasn't lost on me. I couldn't escape him. What did he want from me? I'm no fulminologist, I wanted to tell him. Not anymore. I can't see what's coming until it's too late.

It hits me when it always does, when I go to the bathroom and look in the mirror and can't seem to look myself straight in the eye. I think I'm officially drunk. Today, it's been ten years. *How do you picture your life ten years from now? Do you have kids? Do I have kids?* There are too many things I'll never know.

I push open the door to my old room, to Dean's room, and I enter without turning on the light. I lie down on the bed. The stars are still glowing. A sheet of heat lightning coats the room and I shiver.

Lightning, aneurysms, pregnancies: it's all beyond my control.

I put my hands on my belly and try to stabilize the stars. I stay there for a while, listening to the others clearing the dishes downstairs. My stomach feels strangely full, and it clenches, gripped by a familiar fear. I tell myself lightning can't strike a third time. And I promise him this: if it doesn't, I'll name it Dean.

Somewhere

"Turn here," he says.

She turns. Her knuckles strain the black leather of her gloves as she grasps the wheel, cultivating fluidity as she steers. She's had her licence for a year now and she's finally learning to enjoy the feeling of power over the vehicle.

In the passenger seat, Chip McKay fishes a bottle of Moosehead from a pocket hidden deep in his parka. He takes a swig, eyes on her. It's so cold in the car she can see his breath when he lets out a belch.

It had been Chip's idea to go for a drive after their shift. At least, she wants to let him think it was. She counted the cash while he did a sloppy job of mopping the floor, then they got into her mother's red Cavalier. Now they're driving the long road that circles the airport. Cops out here. Chip McKay wants to see how far he can push her, and she's certainly not going to be the first to swerve.

Katie and Chip have never spoken at school. He comes from the other side of the river, from a neighbourhood she knows mostly as a place kids sometimes go to score booze or harder substances late at night. But you wouldn't know it to look at him:

he doesn't have the hard edges of other guys she's met from that neighbourhood, his eyes open and warm, unguarded. He carries himself with confidence, looks you in the eye and treats you to his wry grin as he runs a hand through his black curls. All this makes a lot of girls at school take notice, but she'd never seen his appeal until she found herself facing his smile from the other side of the prep station at work. She saw the response her presence inspired in his eyes, the way they widened slightly and bloomed. I can use that, she thought. That's something I can work with.

She used to think she knew how to deal with boys like Chip McKay, boys who thought they knew how to get what they wanted from a girl. But Dylan had proved that she didn't, not really. He'd gotten what he'd wanted from her even when she hadn't wanted him to. He'd forced his way in. After that, she'd stopped going out so much. She didn't want to give anything of herself to anyone. She spent a lot of time in her room, on her laptop, delving into the secret worlds she found on the internet. On the net, she was just a collection of letters, phrases strung together, no body, no gender even. She logged on to chat rooms with deliberately androgynous handles.

Alone in her room, emboldened by her internet friends, she'd felt her anger grow into something that felt tangible. Now, after a year, she's ready to be back in the world. Best to dive right in, she's decided. She needs to face what she fears, throw herself into the deep end. Now she's older, maybe wiser, but out of practice. And the stakes feel higher: boys more like men, ambitions wider. The threat of sex underpinning what she'd previously taken to be innocent exchanges.

A guy in her homeroom, Troy, had been killed in a car accident on the way home from a school dance a few weeks ago. A head-on collision with a McCain fries truck. Troy was alone in the car. He'd been drinking—he and his friends always snuck in spiked bottles of Coke to make the dance worth attending. She saw him dancing with Amanda during the last song of the evening, Amanda's red-streaked head nestled against his bleached blond one. She hadn't seen him after that.

Amanda was also in her homeroom, which was actually half-classroom, half-garage: the shop class. Amanda had been cutting class a lot since the accident. The teacher never said anything about the two empty desks, just made a note on the attendance sheet from the front of the class and then stood awkwardly at half-attention while the national anthem played over the loudspeaker. As soon as it ended he strolled past their desk into the garage. Released back into his natural habitat, he puttered under the hood of the 1975 Pontiac Grand Am that had been there for as long as anyone could remember. She wondered if he'd ever render it drivable.

She hadn't known Troy that well, and she'd never thought much about him, but she couldn't wrap her head around the idea of him being gone. Really gone. It just didn't make sense, that he'd been at the desk in front of her on Friday morning and gone on Monday morning. Just as they were on the cusp of real life, about to leave high school. And he'd forever be a high school student. How horrible.

She keeps driving, past the airport and its beckoning lights, its escape routes, past the security guards and the cops, and back into the dark. Chip at least has the decency to lower the beer bottle when they pass the cops. She turns back onto the main road.

Chip laughs. A bellowing sort of laugh, hollow, that fills the car with something that feels false.

"You were a little nervous back there, huh?"

She shakes her head. He reaches a hand toward her and gives her shoulder a squeeze.

"You need to learn how to relax, girl," he says.

"I'm relaxed."

He laughs again.

"I didn't know if a girl like you would be into a guy like me," he says.

She keeps her eyes on the road.

"Let me drive," says Chip.

She pulls over and stops the car.

Katie would be starting university before long, and her mother said she had to make her own way in the world, which meant paying her own way.

"You're a woman now," her mother said, "not a girl."

Of course she rolled her eyes at that, but she also went to the Greek restaurant up the hill and got a job. She served pitas dripping with tzatziki sauce and explained to the customers that, yes, the fries were supposed to be inside the pita. That's how they eat them in Greece. Extra sauce on the side for some customers, the greedy ones. Customers who winked at her and patted her on the ass, gross old men. But sweet ones, too, who called her "dear." A couple in their eighties who came in every Saturday night and split a souvlaki platter with a glass of white wine each.

Technically the manager was supposed to serve the wine, she still being underage, but Jennifer, a chunky, dark-haired woman in her thirties, spent most of her time in the supply closet, the phone cord stretched around the corner and under the closet door.

"Get it yourself," Jennifer finally told her one night after she'd knocked one too many times. "Open the screw cap, pour it into a glass. Not hard. Just ask if they want red or white."

They got free food, the only perk. This was convenient, because in between school, studying, and working shifts, she didn't have much time for meals. Her mother wasn't usually home in the evenings anyway. She was over at Jim's, their neighbour, eating chicken wings or pizza, drinking beer and watching baseball or hockey, depending on the season. She didn't understand why her mother and Jim didn't just move in together, but it never seemed to come up. And it's not like she wanted to live with Jim. He managed a meat market in town and the smell of animal blood that exuded from him was worse than the slick-haired boys at school who doused themselves in cheap cologne, worse than the greasy smell she washed out of her own hair after each shift.

She had begun to feel the fries, the pita, the greasy chicken skewers and tzatziki going to her hips, her thighs, and especially settling around her middle. But the taste of Chip McKay's freshly grilled pita, just enough char marks so it was crispy on the outside but soft and doughy on the inside, dipped into garlic-laced, extra creamy tzatziki sauce? Pure comfort. That's what she looked forward to while trying to stay awake in calculus, her last class of the day. It had nothing to do with Chip McKay himself.

She gets out of the car and Chip gets into the driver's seat. She knows, of course, that this is a bad idea, letting Chip McKay drive her mother's still relatively new Cavalier, and it's not that she trusts Chip, not at all. But there's something about surrendering, the way it makes her feel. Exhilarated, breezy, out of control in a way that's like taking control. She feels free, drunk on it almost, for the first time in months. She sinks into the passenger seat and looks out at the frozen river as Chip drives across the bridge. Even at this time of year, the coldest, there are patches of black where you could fall in if you tried to walk across.

They follow the riverbank, passing the biggest houses in town, imposing and cold in the dark, unlit as if uninhabited, white and ghostly, shadowed against the purer snow.

"Who do you think actually lives there?" she asks.

"The usual rich people. Politicians, heads of companies, lawyers, doctors," he says.

Chip McKay's family isn't rich, she knows that much. He actually needs to work, and not just to save for university, unlike her friends at school. If she thinks about it, she doesn't really know anything about Chip McKay: what drives him, what he wants to do with his life. He mocks her attempts at unearthing biographical information, as if the mundane nature of this line of questioning betrays her bourgeois upbringing. Her upbringing wasn't exactly that bourgeois, but she knows he sees her that way.

"You're way too polite," he told her once, after some customer yelled at her because the meat in his pita wasn't hot enough. "People are going to walk all over you some day."

"Well," she said, "let's hope they're not wearing stilettos."

"Does anyone wear stilettos in this shithole of a town?" he scoffed.

"Who said I was staying here?"

"Where are you going?"

"Toronto. That's why I'm working here. To save up. Well, first for university, and then to move to Toronto."

89

"Oh yeah?"

She could tell he didn't believe her. He'd surely seen too many small-time girls blow through, waitressing on their way toward pipe dreams. How's he supposed to know she's different? He doesn't know the first thing about her. He just sees the increasingly stained ugly white polyester shirt and black skirt she wears to work every night, her messy ponytail, her tired eyes lined by black eyeliner that's always smudged by the end of the night. He sees the relish with which she consumes the pita he grills for her, her sloppy tzatziki-covered mouth. He sees her jittery hands, her tapping foot, her finger twirling the depths of her ponytail.

"Your boyfriend not giving you any, or what?" he asked one night.

Her neck turned so fast a pain shot up the side of it.

"What?"

"You're super tense, girl. Relax a little. The customers will like you better that way. You'll get more tips."

Nothing like someone telling her to relax to make her even more anxious.

"You want to move to Toronto, or what?" he asked.

She picked up two big combo plates from the middle shelf, avoiding his eyes. A fry slipped off one of the plates and she cursed.

"Whoa, there," laughed Chip. "Calm down, girl."

She scowled and rolled her eyes, but reset her expression before she went through the swinging doors.

"Here you go, two souvlaki platters," she chirped as she set the plates in front of two middle-aged men, regulars.

"Thanks, honey," said one, giving her a pat that was dangerously close to her ass.

"Pleasure," she said.

"So, hon," said the other. "When are you due?"

"Due?"

She stared at him.

"The baby?"

"There's no baby."

She flushed and fled back into the kitchen. Bypassing Chip's eyes, she locked herself in the employee bathroom. She caught sight of herself in the required white shirt, its clingy polyester fabric. Christ, she really did look pregnant.

After that, she stopped eating Chip's pita. She stopped eating much at all.

Chip keeps driving into a part of town she never goes, the eastern-most reaches of the city limits. A few turns, and he pulls into a driveway.

"Stay here," he says.

He gets out of the car. She watches him plod up the steps that haven't been shovelled and knock on a paint-peeled door that presumably used to be white. A guy in a cowboy hat and no shirt answers, then disappears while Chip waits outside. He opens the door again a few minutes later, and the exchange is too quick for her to see.

Chip gets back into the car and pulls out of the driveway without a word. She catches a glimpse of a bottle before it disappears into his parka. She wonders how much he's had to drink tonight. He looks steady, but you never know.

Chip McKay is a drinker, this much she knows. When the bell rings and she goes to pick up plates, she sees him on the other side of the metal shelving at the prep station, sneaking sips from a flask he keeps in the pocket of his white chef coat. He winks at her when he catches her looking. He's two years older, meaning he's eighteen or nineteen, depending on his birthday. He got held back a couple of years in school. She wonders if he'll graduate this year. She has no idea what classes he's taking this term, nor how often he actually shows up.

Her heart is set on university, hence the job. University, she knows, is her ticket out of here. She plans to do a couple of years in town, keep saving money on the side, then get a scholarship and transfer somewhere else. She wants to take computer science. Computers make sense to her, always have, and she likes tinkering on them, solving problems. Logical stuff. She's been teaching herself to code, spending long nights in chat rooms conversing with programmers and hackers. She'd even enrolled in a computer science class this term. But on the first day, she was walking toward the class and spotted Dylan ahead of her. When he turned into the classroom, she knew she couldn't do it. She peeked into the window as she walked by. All guys, every one of them. She dropped the class and took creative writing instead. She could teach herself to code.

"Isn't that kind of a guy thing?" her mother said when she mentioned computer science.

But Katie didn't care. There was money in it. And she had the grades to get in.

Chip reaches into his parka and pulls out the bottle, passing it to her. It's brown, slim, with no label. She has no idea what's inside.

"C'mon, just take a sip," he says.

She puts it to her lips and pretends to take a sip.

92

Chip laughs.

"Girl, I can see right through you."

She's irritated. Suddenly she no longer wants to be trapped in this car with Chip McKay. Her plan seems silly. Maybe she's not so ready for this, after all.

"Take me home," she tells him.

"Nah," he says.

"I want to go home."

"No, you don't."

"Yes, I do."

She tries to sound forceful, like she and her mother have talked about.

"C'mon babe, relax. We're just going for a drive. You don't have to drink anything."

He takes the bottle back from her and snugs it between his legs. They drive, not talking.

She wonders what Chip would taste like. Beer, sweat, tzatziki sauce, whiskey. He looks over, as if he has read her mind, and grins.

"What 'ya thinking, blondie?"

"Nothing."

"I think you want a swig off my bottle, don't you?"

He pulls over to the side of the road. They're really in the middle of nowhere now, surrounded only by trees. It's so dark she can't see anything beyond the arc of the headlights. He pulls the bottle out of his jacket. This time, she takes a sip. It burns her throat and she coughs.

"Strong stuff, huh?"

"Yeah," is all she can manage.

He grabs it back from her and takes a long gulp.

Chip looks at her, his expression unreadable. She draws herself into her bulky coat, shivering. He reaches over and traces a finger down the side of her face, tucks a loose strand of hair into her coat collar.

Chip undoes his seat belt, then his belt. She stares at the darkness in front of her. Chip reaches for her and pulls her toward him. She stays still, not struggling, but not surrendering, either. She reminds herself that this is where she needs him, that this is what she wanted. He doesn't kiss her, though, but instead pushes her head downward, slipping his pants away with surprising fluidity. It feels all wrong, at first, to have her mouth around him. Awkward and dry, this foreign fleshy object in her mouth. She coughs, trying not to choke. But eventually she falls into a familiar rhythm.

She'd been in this same car with Dylan, when it still reeked of the new car smell that has since been tempered by fries and garlic. He wasn't anything like Chip. Quiet, occasionally flashing eyes that were otherwise dull and grey. He had nothing of Chip's confidence, either. She'd had to make the first move. You would have thought he'd be sweet with girls. He didn't seem like the type. His was a quiet rage, but once unleashed it was fatal.

Chip is gasping and when she feels him about to come she pulls away. He grabs a Kleenex from his pocket.

"You're one of those, huh? No swallowing?"

She shrugs, unable to look at him.

"Whatever," he says, and starts the car.

She leans her head back against the seat, facing the window so she doesn't have to look at him. What would have happened if she'd said no?

She'd tried to say no, with Dylan, and look at where that had gotten her. Her mother hadn't let her go to school for a week. She said it was better for them to deal with it their own way, at home. She didn't want people to wonder about the bruises, to ask the wrong questions. But her homeroom teacher hadn't asked any questions when she'd returned to school. No one had.

This time, she hadn't wanted to say no. But it wasn't what she'd imagined. There'd been no pleasure. Not for her.

Chip starts the car again and drives. The streetlights don't make a dent in the big envelope of darkness.

"Where are we?" she asks.

"Somewhere," he says.

"Turn right," she says, when they come to an intersection.

"Why?"

"Because."

That road is as black as the last. She wonders what Troy was looking at, in those last moments before the crash. What had he been thinking? Was he on a road as black as this one?

Chip takes the flask out of his pocket and is taking a swig when she hears a thud. It starts outside the car, until it's in her ear, beside her.

"What was that?"

"What was what?"

"That. The noise. Didn't you hear it?"

"No."

"Stop!"

"Hey, calm down."

"Let me out of the car."

95

"Come on, chill."

"Chip McKay, let me out of this car!"

He finally stops. She gets out and waits as her eyes adjust to the darkness. She sees it, behind them, a dark, furry shape on the road, a flash of white. At least it's not human. But when she comes upon it, she wants to cry. A deer. A young one, from the looks of it, skinny legs splayed at a deadly angle.

She feels hands on her shoulders. Chip.

"You killed it."

"I didn't mean to."

"With my car."

She doesn't remember kneeling, but next thing she knows she's sitting down on the road, hands on the deer's quickly cooling coat. It feels silky under her fingers. She closes her eyes.

"Katie, you can't bring it back to life."

"I know," she says softly.

"C'mon, let's go, before someone comes."

"No, we have to do something with it."

"Do what?"

"I don't know. Bury it?"

"Katie!"

The urgency in his voice makes her look up. He points at the headlights in the distance.

"Get in. Now!"

She gets up, intending to obey, but then she looks at Chip and back at the deer, and she stops. She sits back down.

Chip drives off. She lets him go.

She keeps her hands on the deer's fur and protects him against the sweep of lights coming their way.

Brothers

It happens in an instant, in the middle of the night. An accident.

Wanting to stay as close to sleep as possible, she doesn't turn on any lights. Only a few quick quiet steps to reach the bathroom. Sit down, stand up, rinse. Squeaks approaching her on the old wooden floorboards. Her husband, Andy.

The dark hallway so narrow their shoulders brush together as they come upon each other. She reaches her hand along his shoulder to his neck, offhandedly sultry in her sleepiness. Then they're kissing. His mouth different, softer and wetter, saltier. Her lips bloom in response, her closed eyelids tingle. She starts to wake up as a tremor runs up her thigh, a strangely unfamiliar sensation. Her hand to his face, more whiskered than it should be. Something opens inside her and spreads, startling in its intensity, like the juice that leaks out of a pomegranate and stains everything in its path. His kiss unusually urgent, layered. The texture of a fresh fig.

Her belly between them.

She opens her eyes, which are adjusting to the darkness. Andy's brother Marc, visiting from New York.

Marc is the same height as Andy, but everything else about them is different. Andy is fair while Marc is dark. Andy barely needs to shave while Marc can grow a beard overnight. Andy is taut and lean. Marc is filled out, firm, muscled.

It takes longer than it should for the message to transfer from her head to her lips, from her lips to her hands, which are cupping Marc's butt cheeks.

She removes her hands, removes her lips, feels the redness of her face though no one can see it. She pushes Marc's hand away.

Without a word, she continues down the hall into the bedroom where Andy is sleeping, mouth open in a frozen yawn. The bed smells like sleep, and she falls into it, now fully awake.

Andy's side of the bed is empty when she wakes up the next morning. Her chest seizes with fear, but then his laughter wafts up through the floorboards, chased by Marc's booming voice. Andy and Marc have always been close. Grace, an only child, wonders what it must be like, to face the adult world in the companionship of someone shaped by the same constellation of early childhood memories.

Marc drove up from New York on a whim and showed up unannounced, hopped up on Twizzlers and machine-sweetened cappuccinos from roadside convenience stores. Knowing that last-minute houseguests make her anxious, Andy was quick to set up the spare room. But what really bothers her is the change that comes over Andy when Marc is around, almost like he's deliberately excluding her, as if she's too far outside the Venn diagram of his and Marc's shared experience. She hates the way Andy dances around her, doting on her like he would an ageing grandmother, waiting for her to go away so the real fun can begin.

"Morning, Grace," says Marc, as her bare feet slap down the dark wooded steps that descend into the kitchen.

She feels his eyes, the heat rising in her face. Is he not a little too eager, greeting her even before her husband? She keeps her mouth shut, pressing her lips together to stop them from trembling.

Andy kisses her on the cheek. When he moves away she catches sight of her reflection in the mirror on the opposite wall and is surprised by its ugliness. Her face red and pillow creased, her hair pulled back in an unflattering ponytail. Do Andy and Marc see her this way, too?

"Sit down," says Andy, pulling out a chair. "I'll fix you some breakfast."

"There's coffee," says Marc. "Beans from Brooklyn. Let me get you a cup."

"Coffee?" Andy says.

Grace can tell he's trying to keep his tone casual.

"I'll skip the coffee," she says.

Ever since the pregnancy, Andy handles her with kid gloves, wanting to take care of her all the time. He often calls on the way home from work.

"Any cravings? I can pick something up."

Everyone expects her to have cravings, but so far, nothing. Just the opposite: most food disgusts her, except bananas, which she doesn't exactly crave but tolerates more than most things. They have just the right balance between blandness and flavour. Andy would slice one up for her, smearing each bite with a tiny dab of peanut butter and arranging it on a white porcelain plate. His gestures are sweet, a preparation for fatherhood, but it's as if he doesn't quite trust her to take care of their baby even while it's still in the womb.

"A cup of coffee never hurt anyone," Marc says.

Andy shrugs.

"Better safe than sorry."

"Say those who never have any fun in life, ever," Marc laughs.

Andy keeps his eyes on the stove, waiting for the water to boil so he can make her a poached egg (healthier than fried, he maintains). The sunlight streams through the window and hits the side of Grace's face, making her squint.

Grace came from Truro, Nova Scotia. The town had a nickname—Hubtown—that had made her want to distance herself from it. She'd moved to Toronto as soon as she was old enough to leave her parents' house. The juxtapositions of Toronto excited her: the grittiness of her Chinatown neighbourhood late at night when cartons of mangos and leftover vegetables perfumed the street, the stately elegance of her leafy university campus and its storied buildings, its anachronistic formality. During her first few years in Toronto Grace rarely spoke, simply taking it all in. She studied film and spent most of her free time in front of a screen. She lived her life like that, too. Observing. Forgetting life wasn't a film. Holing up in coffee shops and taking notes on what she saw, details for her future screenplay.

Grace didn't usually need other people, not then, but occasionally she wanted to feel another body against hers. When that happened, she went to a bar. She ordered a whiskey on the rocks and let it sit in front of her until it had been diluted beyond repair. She didn't need to say much. The less said, the better. She met indie rock guys in sleeveless plaid shirts who wanted to talk about their band and their ideas and didn't seem to care who was listening as long as someone was. When they asked for her number she wrote it on their arms, below the tattoos, altering only the last digit.

She was giving a guy named Pete a blowjob in his shitty studio apartment above a goth club when it finally hit her. Pure revulsion. She withdrew her mouth and left Pete's apartment, clattering down the stairs two at a time. His voice echoed after her, out the window into the empty street. *Ever hear of blue balls, bitch?* Enough, she told herself.

She was twenty-five when she met Andy. Post-university, they had both been hired as temps to screen incoming hospital patients for signs of severe acute respiratory syndrome. Her shift started at 6:30 A.M., an unprecedented hour for Grace. But she came to look forward to her early morning bike ride, the air still fresh before the rise of the day's humidity, the serene streets unclogged by cranky commuters. At the hospital, the quiet extended for an hour on good days, everyone sleepily clutching the cups that would ferry them through their morning. The SARS crisis was tapering off.

Her job was to stand at the door with a squirt bottle and give each visitor their prescribed glob of hand sanitizer. On her first day, she accidentally delivered a sanitizing dollop to her favourite skirt, a green, triangular number with flowers embroidered into the bottom right corner. The bleached blob defied her frantic scrubbing in the tiny employee bathroom and developed into an unfortunate penis-shaped stain. She believed in omens, and this seemed like an ominous one. But at the end of that day, she met Andy. He was replacing her, com-

101

ing on for the late afternoon shift. He had spiky blond hair and a surfer tan that made his green eyes stand out from the rest of his face. He wasn't anything like the guys she usually met, with his long shorts and Velcro flip-flops that made him look like he was ready for a game of beach volleyball, and she liked that.

He shook her hand and introduced himself while taking the bottle of hand sanitizer from her other hand. His eyes fell to her skirt.

"Maybe you should work on your aim if you're going to wear such pretty skirts to the hospital."

She laughed.

"I was a pitcher in the Little League. Maybe I could give you some tips," he said.

He wagged his eyebrows at her, spun the bottle of sanitizer and tucked it against his hip like he was putting a gun in a holster.

When she got home she wrote a scene based on their meeting. She moulded it, shaping Andy's dialogue. Under her pen he became much wittier than he had, in fact, been.

Their temp agency specialized in employing out-of-work artists, and as an aspiring screenwriter, Grace fit right in. She was between scripts and went home to watch movies every afternoon after she got off at the hospital. Andy, on the other hand, harboured no illusions about the realities of moneymaking, and had no intention of pursuing art seriously. He'd done a general arts degree, majoring in philosophy, and was considering applying to law school. But first, he wanted to take a break.

Andy came in to replace her one day only to be told they didn't need him anymore. After no new cases of SARS for thirty days, the restrictions were lifted, and the hospital was downsizing its temporary staff. He shrugged at the news and walked out of the building with her. As they left the clinical hospital coolness, a wave of July heat came up to greet them as if someone had turned on a giant blow dryer.

"Guess that means my night is free after all," he said.

"I was planning to go to a movie ..." she said. "The theatre is air-conditioned."

"Is that an invitation?"

"Do you want it to be one?"

Andy suggested they see *My Life Without Me* at the Carlton. In it, Sarah Polley is living in a trailer in her mother's garden with her husband Scott Speedman and their two kids when she's diagnosed with cancer and told she has two months to live. She doesn't tell anyone she has cancer, and she has an affair with Mark Ruffalo even though she loves her husband.

All through the movie, Grace was acutely aware of Andy's arm on the armrest beside hers. By the end of the movie, their arms were touching.

"She was pretty selfish, really," Andy said when they left the theatre.

Grace shrugged, still in her head, not ready to speak and break the bittersweet mood the film had washed over her.

"I just don't get people who cheat," he continued. "Who would do that to someone they love?"

Grace didn't think things were so black and white. There were always twists, the wrenches life threw at you. Like cancer. But she didn't say this.

Andy reached for her hand as they crossed the street. He later confessed that he usually only went to see big blockbusters.

Grace was let go from the hospital a week later, and she and Andy spent the rest of the summer together. Andy's lightness of being rubbed off on her, and for the first time, she didn't worry about money, didn't worry about getting another job. Instead, she just *was*. On Bloor Street, they sat on a patio drinking sugar-laden sangria and watched as the lazy afternoon crowd picked up into buzzing after-work types, the light fading and the unseasonal Christmas lights twinkling on around them as they ordered a slice of cake to share and stayed on past dinner. They got hyped up on frappés and licked each other's tzatziki-drenched fingers on the Danforth. Andy laughed at her dorky kneepads when they went rollerblading in the Beaches, but he recanted when he tripped on a takeout coffee cup and flew into the boardwalk, knees first. He hadn't done much rollerblading, he admitted.

Grace's apartment was in Chinatown, which had become much quieter since the SARS outbreak. People rushed through the streets with masks covering their faces to avoid any potential contagion. She and Andy decided to try a new fruit each day (they agreed on their favourite, mangosteen, but were divided on durian: Andy found it foul, Grace found it sumptuous), until all the Chinatown fruit was familiar and they had to move on. They went hiking in High Park, which was when Grace learned that despite his appearance, Andy didn't have an athletic bone in his body. He wheezed after mere steps up a hill. But the joke was on her when Andy had to give her a second skin of calamine lotion that night to soothe all the angry mosquito welts.

Through it all, they watched many, many movies. They didn't discriminate: it might be Fellini one day, but Schwarzenegger the next. Andy's favourite movie was *Kindergarten Cop*, and Grace was less than successful in not making fun of this.

When she was around Andy, Grace's jaw ached at the end of the day from so much grinning. The few friends she'd kept from school remarked on it: how different she seemed, how relaxed. During her last two years of university, she'd hardly looked up from her books or her laptop, too worried about her grades for any real kind of social life. And for what? Instead, now, this unfamiliar feeling, this elation. Maybe this was what being happy felt like.

Andy often talked about his brother. Marc lived in Germany, where he'd moved after his wife Camille got a job with a big designer in Berlin, and the time difference reduced Marc and Andy's communication to email. Grace picked up the phone one day, the first time she heard Marc's voice. She remarked on its bass smoothness, so different from Andy's laugh-soaked alto. Marc's was a voice of concealed depth.

"I'll see you soon," Marc said to Grace.

"Two things," Marc told Andy when he picked up. "One: I'm coming home. Two: Camille and I are through."

Grace prepared herself for a depressed brother, for evenings spent consoling him, building up his morale like in one of those romantic comedies (though not the type of film she would ever write). Camille and Marc had married so young. How would he face adult life without her?

She was surprised by Marc's confidence, his good looks, his swagger. The charisma that surrounded him like a force field. This did not seem like a man whose wife cheats.

"I was tired of Berlin," Marc told them. "I tried to learn German, but it just didn't stick."

"And Camille?" Andy asked.

"She'll stay there, with the Berliner. He's a nice guy, actually. Intelligent. Good taste in music. Without him I never would have found the best coffee in Berlin."

Andy raised his eyebrows at this.

"People aren't so hung up on monogamy there," Marc said. "None of our friends were married."

Andy rolled his eyes. His tolerance for what he called "boho affectations" had decreased as he'd aged.

"Besides," Marc said, "when you've been with someone since high school, you eventually need a change."

Marc's presence shifted the energy in the house: what previously had been static was now swirling, frantic. Marc wasn't someone who could sit still. They tried peanut dumplings at the new dim sum place around the corner, a post-feminist art exhibit at the local gallery, a punk show in Kensington market, a Surrealist lecture at the museum. Marc didn't seem to mind what they were doing as long as they were doing something. Grace and Andy competed to see who could come up with the best activities. Grace was the one who found the slow dance party, but she felt a twinge of regret when she saw Marc arm-in-arm with a young, pretty blonde whose arms were sleeved in tattoos.

Every so often, Grace was startled by a shadow that passed across Marc's face, an expression that made him look wholly unlike himself. It was like driving through a tunnel on a bright day. Sometimes he held her gaze for a beat too long, and she felt something in her chest start to unravel. But she'd blink and his features resolidified into the playful disposition she'd come to know. Almost always.

Marc had been with them for a month when they came

home to a note left atop carefully folded blankets. Marc had decided that change meant leaving his hometown, that change meant New York.

Grace was disconcerted by the hole Marc's absence left in her marriage. With him around, things had felt magnified, with the startling fresh colours that follow a rainfall. The constant swirl of activities, of newness, reminded her of when she and Andy first started dating, back when she still felt things. When did the numbness take over? It spread slowly, almost imperceptibly, seeping into her marriage. She hadn't appreciated the vibrancy of her twenties while she still had them. In her thirties, everything was dull, muted. In their thirties, she and Andy were like two planets orbiting the same star in opposite directions, only occasionally coming into contact. When she thought about this too much, her bones ached.

Andy didn't seem to notice. He was happy to return his focus to work. He worked long hours, even going in on weekends to prepare for trials, hoping he might get a shot at partner. During dinner he recounted his cases in excruciating detail, until Grace used the dishes as an excuse to get up. But at least he was passionate about his work. She, on the other hand, hadn't tried to write a script in a long time. She couldn't even remember the last time she'd watched a movie.

Although he wouldn't admit it, she knew Andy had been relieved when she'd finally taken a permanent job as a receptionist at the hospital, the same one where they'd first met several years before. Once she turned thirty, temping seemed déclassé. Besides, she liked being around patients. It was easy to see her good fortune in comparison.

Andy had solidified as he'd gotten older, his skater shorts swapped for slacks and his flip-flops replaced by shoes that required shining. He lost his surfer-like tan and let his bleached blond hair fade back to its natural red. Law school agreed with him; his shoulders straightened, his posture improved. Faced with his new confidence, Grace felt herself slowly slipping into his shadow. To her embarrassment, she became comfortable there. Andy's wife.

Andy's life before they'd met remained opaque. He never talked about ex-girlfriends, something that, when they met, Grace found suspicious.

"I don't think there were any others, before you," Marc finally told her. "At least none that I knew of."

This surprised her. Andy was charming; he'd courted her with what seemed like experience. Maybe it ran in the family. In his new New York life, Marc seemed to be on a date with a new girl each week. Grace rooted for the pharmacist from New Brunswick with a baby face and sweet Maritime accent, but Marc broke it off with her for an art school dropout from Cleveland, a red-haired painter much too young for him, a girl who, in the photos Marc sent, always had a cigarette dangling from lips or limb. Sometimes she held it with her toes while she painted, Marc told them.

Grace found out about the pregnancy after Marc's departure. A small hope ignited inside her, and for a few weeks she and Andy carried themselves on this spark. Andy came home earlier. He made Shirley Temples and they sat on the balcony eating yellow watermelon and spitting seeds off the side while discussing baby names. The only names Grace could come up with were ones she'd already given characters in her screenplays.

All of Andy's names sounded too grandiose, too recklessly hopeful about their baby's future: Darwin, Lincoln, Hemingway, Socrates, Newton. She could never tell if he was joking. Also: all boy names.

Andy was late coming home one night. She went down the street to a bar and ordered a whiskey on the rocks. She was still barely showing. She took out her notebook and started writing. She found herself writing a character who resembled Marc, angling to capture his charisma. She sat there for hours before the bartender eyed her watery whiskey dubiously and asked if she wanted another.

Her script was no good. But at least she was writing again. She'd missed it, especially dialogue, her favourite part. When her scripts were critiqued in her last screenwriting workshop, the other students said she made her characters speak too philosophically. It wasn't realistic, they said. Too much dialogue: big, fat, black chunks of dense text. Apparently they hadn't watched many French films. This new script of hers had almost no dialogue, just action.

Watching Marc, Grace sees that her portrayal wasn't entirely accurate. He leaves a trail of dirty dishes and coffee grinds in his wake; in real life he is too clumsy for the fluid, decisive movements of her character. Andy, on the other hand, has become the neatest man Grace has ever met. He makes their bed every morning without fail, even replacing the throw pillows that would have ended up in the closet had she been on her own. Whenever she tries to make the bed it ends up looking lumpy, nothing like his perfect corners. Before he leaves for work, he washes the dishes and wipes the counters, then sweeps through the house to open the windows and put doorstops under the doors to keep them open in the breeze. He feels a house should have constant air and light moving through it. Sometimes Grace leaves a dirty plate out just to see how long it will last.

Even now, a Saturday morning, Andy is busy cleaning as he goes, wiping down the counter as he waits for her egg to cook.

"I think it's clean, dude," Marc says.

Marc sits down across from Grace and watches her sip a glass of lemon water, his gaze level. Her lips burn. She can't look at him. She brings her fingers to her lips, then quickly moves her hand back to the table, worried that Marc can tell what she's thinking.

She should be researching products, buying things for the baby, but she can't bring herself to care about mommy blogs or books or shops. They decided not to find out the sex; Andy wanted to be surprised. But now she can't get out of the habit of thinking of the baby as "it." Maybe it will hit her later, she keeps thinking. Later. And still later. For the time being, she feels justified in eating full-fat yogurt, an indulgence she's never allowed herself.

Motherhood is expected of her. Yet the thing growing inside her feels foreign, a world apart. Like an out-of-body experience contained within her, a separate world she can observe without feeling its connection to her. It's kicking now, she thinks. It's hungry. It's sad.

Sadness is something she can observe in it, a small clench of its body like a fist, and that is the one feeling that affects her more than the others. It washes over her, strangely pleasurable, like the climax of a cramp just before it dissipates. She knows that her own baby's sadness is not something she should take pleasure in. But it's comforting in the way that watching *Dancer in the Dark* had been comforting. As she'd sobbed, the negative emotion had drained out with the tears, and when she was done she felt more at peace than she had in a long time.

These are the things she can't tell Andy, the things that would make his face screw up in distaste. His forehead wrinkles unattractively when she tries to explain the way she feels. Better to skip the coffee and let him make her breakfast.

She eats her egg, taking careful, tiny bites and keeping her eyes on her plate. Marc sips at his coffee, waving his hands as he recounts some childhood memory. She isn't listening. She prefers to let them reminisce. No need for her to participate, no way she can compete with their brotherly bond that has a tendency to run off through a sun-lit field, leaving her behind in her basement of thoughts.

She idly wonders if it's possible the baby could inherit Marc's penchant for facial hair, his long arms. She takes her plate to the sink and watches as Andy and Marc continue talking and laughing, arms waving. Andy looks so boyish next to Marc's ruggedness, so light and fragile, like he could be knocked over by one of Marc's arms if he wasn't careful. She turns away to rinse her plate.

It's only a second too long, but when Marc's touch warms the small of her back, she knows last night wasn't a dream. She avoids his gaze, busying herself with wiping down the counter Andy has already cleaned. As Marc stands beside her at the sink, she feels the warmth emanating from his body and finds herself sneaking a glance at his arms, the way the muscles strain against his black T-shirt. She imagines the smoothness of his chest underneath. If she had another chance, would she?

Marc returns to the table to sit with Andy.

Just then she feels a kick, as if the baby is announcing itself, reining her in. As if the baby is her conscience. She pictures the baby as a little angel and a little devil, one on each of her shoulders, and gives them Andy's red hair and now-pale skin. She laughs out loud. Of course, she would never. She couldn't. She wouldn't.

Rituals

The night we arrive in Pune it rains harder than I've ever seen it rain, so hard Matt jokes the gods must be pissed about our arrival. We're in a restaurant near our hotel when it starts. I eat dark dal makhani swirled with white streaks of yogurt raita, and Matt eats murgh korma, chicken curry on rice. The rain persists. Food finished, bill paid, we're dismissed with a polite head bob. We loiter uncertainly in the doorway of the restaurant, then we make a run for it.

We only get as far as the security booth that separates the building from the street, where guards laze around listening to the radio. They wave us in, turn down the music so we can listen to the rain thumping against cheap plastic windows that do not seem up to the task of standing up to this god-like rain.

It doesn't stop, and our presence in the booth begins to feel like an embarrassing imposition, a breach of something as yet unknown to me. Matt and I wade through the gushing brown brook that used to pass for a sidewalk, letting the water rush over our feet. Three blocks feels like a day in the time of Noah. When we enter our hotel, the sudden coolness gives me goose bumps. My hair is plastered against my skull. I feel my underwear sticking to me underneath my clothes as water drips onto the polished marble floor of the lobby. All the guests in their suits and sparkling saris stare at us from the adjoining bar as we squeak across the lobby.

Matt looks at me and down at the water dripping on the floor. He bursts out laughing. I smile weakly. He guides me toward the elevator, rubbing my shoulders and exchanging nods with a hotel porter as we pass. We go to the room, strip, and get in the shower together. I turn my face away from him, toward the warm jet of water. He massages the back of my neck and I lean in to him, almost falling asleep. Jet lag.

It rains every day our first week in India. The monsoon was supposed to be over when we arrived, but it's late this year. Matt's been to India many times for work, and he swears it's not normally like this. Our waiter at breakfast says we arrived just in time for the heaviest rain this monsoon. I try to learn the phraseology of monsoons, to say "this monsoon" like I'd say "this spring" back home.

Before Matt leaves for the office, he says I can make use of his driver during the day, that he'll take me anywhere. The thought of someone waiting in the hot car while I visit a tourist trap temple is too much. Instead, I stay around the hotel. I could leave on foot, but there are no real sidewalks and the unruly traffic spreads to cover every available surface.

Besides, the pollution isn't good for my skin, which is getting worse. I go to the hotel spa for a facial and charge it to the room. Layer after layer of thick, cool cream soothes my skin. Back in the room, I close the curtains and lie on the bed face up, making sure my face doesn't touch the pillow.

It's not like I haven't travelled before—I did the requisite

European backpacking trip and spent a year teaching English in Japan in my twenties—but there's something about India that gives me pause. India had often been in the news shortly before our trip, after a woman had been brutally beaten and raped on a bus by a gang of men. Though I try not to buy into the media hype and let a single case influence the way I see an entire country, I am nervous.

That weekend we take a short flight to Hyderabad, because it's close enough and Matt hasn't been there yet. We go to the Golconda Fort and wander through the ruins that make up the complex, passing through courtyards and gardens, climbing higher and higher, our footsteps echoing off crumbling walls. When Matt wants to go to an unsheltered lookout at the very top, I elect to stay behind due to the 40°c-plus heat. I'm lurking in the shadows to stay cool when a man approaches me.

"People have been watching you," he says, "and I recommend you don't stand here alone. You're a foreigner. Keep moving. Stay safe."

We're the only white tourists around, it occurs to me now. The heat's gone to my head and I panic, rush blindly back toward the entrance, winding my way through darkened chambers and tripping down staircases, texting Matt to meet me ASAP. I receive the usual amount of attention on the way down—a man wanting to take a photo of me with his daughter, random men snapping cell phone pictures when they think I'm not looking—but I focus only on getting to the gate, in view of the guards.

"Your wife went that way," everyone told Matt on his descent, as he recounted later. He didn't even need to ask.

After that, back in Pune, it's even easier to stay in the hotel.

Besides, in my thirties I've become a lazy traveller, one who prizes the comfortable and the familiar. And the hotel we're staying at is both. Huge, a world unto itself. Four restaurants, two bars, that spa, a gym, an indoor and outdoor pool, even a library. At the luxurious breakfast buffet, I point to a new fruit each morning. The boy behind the fruit table slices it open for me, revealing flesh and seeds. He teaches me their names. Custard apple, guava, cherimoya, tamarind, sweet lime, and the sweetest of all, sapota, which tastes like brown sugar. While I am overly conscious that we aren't having an authentic Indian experience, Matt's company is footing the bill for this fancy five-star Western hotel, and I try to make the most of it.

I linger after the driver takes Matt to the office, sipping my chai and—conspicuously I feel, so I hide the cover—reading a memoir by an American writer who spent a few years in India exploring religions, trying on spiritualities like jeans.

"Are you enjoying India, Madam?" asks a server whose light complexion, freckles, and red-hued hair confuse me.

He looks almost Irish, but sounds Indian. His face is a little blotchy. Could he have a skin condition? I feel an immediate affinity toward him.

"Oh, yes," I say.

"Are you here for business or pleasure?"

"Pleasure, I suppose. My husband is here for work."

The white lie slips off my tongue before I have time to think about it. Matt and I aren't married, but here it feels simpler to call him my husband.

"What's your name?" he asks.

"Janice."

"I hope you enjoy India, Madam Janice."

He looks at me with a hint of amusement in his green eyes, and I spend about five seconds wondering what it would be like to have an affair with him. He gives a slight bow and walks away. The thing is, I wouldn't have the first clue about how to initiate an affair. I've always lacked guile.

Most couples have a baby to save their relationship, but we decided on an around-the-world trip. If we can make it through this, I figure, we can make it through life. Plus, the prospect sounded more attractive than sticking around to attend the support group my therapist had been pressuring me to join.

"A change of scenery," Matt said. "That's all you need."

It's not like things had been going well for me career-wise: I'd been on the verge of getting fired. My credit cards were maxed out, my savings depleted.

Matt, on the other hand, had plenty of savings, more than he knew what to do with. He comes from a wealthy family, and he had a good job. He decided we both needed to get away, and he told me not to worry about my inability to contribute. He'd finance the trip, he said, but as a condition, I had to give him my credit card for safekeeping. He didn't know I had another card, the department store Mastercard I received just before leaving. I kept it hidden in the depths of my wallet, promising myself it was only for emergencies. It's not like Matt was obsession-free. He'd had his own promises to make.

The next day is Mahatma Gandhi Day. Also, a dry day, as we discover when Matt tries to order a beer in a Malaysian restaurant. I haven't had a drink since arriving in India, and I sense Matt's relief that I've never taken to beer, the drink of choice here. Matt's never been a big drinker. Beyond a single beer, two at most, he loses interest. Matt is the king of moderation, something that's never been my strong point. I do best with constraints, with extremes: I can't simply "cut down"; I need to cut it out entirely. Matt finds this mystifying. Which is funny, because he should be familiar with extremists. It's in his blood. He grew up in rural Nova Scotia, with a father who was an extremist of a type: an alcoholic, straight up. Scion of a meat delivery business turned national grocery empire. Matt won't talk about it—it took three years to ferret out any details. He's come by his self-restraint honestly; I can't begrudge him that. But my efforts to get him to open up about his past just make him roll his eyes. *What are you, my therapist?* I hear the icy edge creep into his voice and I know to drop it.

That weekend we fly up to Delhi, and in Old Delhi we enter the mosh pit that is the old spice market. Men swivel their heads as we pass, and I duck my eyes to avoid meeting curious stares, keeping my hands in my pockets. The street is a colourful yet dusty mess of cars, bikes, tuktuks, rickshaws, and carts loaded with sack spilling off sack of pulses, grains, and flour. A dark alley blossoms into a bouquet of straw baskets filled with richly-hued spices. I stick my hand into a barrel of dried lentils, looking the other way as if to disassociate myself from my hand in case anyone is offended by its action. My whole arm could get lost in there.

We hire a driver who takes us on a rural highway that winds through small villages where women wearing colourful saris carry large baskets on their heads and men in white uniforms and sailor caps stand together in clusters, eyeing us as we pass. We see a herd of goats being cajoled up the street, and two cows whose horns and face have been dyed neon pink. We watch drivers perform an elaborate dance of avoidance when a cow enters traffic and slowly crosses the road with its head held as high as Cleopatra, a bell around its regal neck. Traffic works differently here, and there are no real lanes. Everyone weaves in and out, crossing from one side to the other in a game of high-speed chicken. Many times I catch my breath as I watch another vehicle come straight for us and get out of the way just in time. You can't avoid the noise: the "Horn O.K. Please" signs painted on the back of trucks are faithfully obeyed, and each vehicle has its unique note. When we finally reach the Taj Mahal, hours later, my head aches from the musical cacophony of the highway.

We're pressured into hiring a tour guide whose speciality is cheesy tourist photos with a twist. He positions us so it looks like I'm standing in Matt's hand, with the majestic architecture as only backdrop. I notice Matt grinning, and I turn to find a growing crowd of small Indian schoolgirls trailing behind me. I smile at them, but they dart away, giggling.

Matt and I both fall asleep on the ride back to Delhi, my head sinking deeper and deeper into his shoulder. I wake up with a crick in my neck. It's late when we get back to the hotel. We take quick showers to rinse off the grime of a day wandering Agra's tourist sites.

I look in the mirror after getting out of the shower. My face looks wrong. Angry bumps, red and protruding, and small, white ones. I fall into a trance, picking and squeezing, coaxing out the impurities and feeling a sweet relief when a tiny squiggle of white emerges.

Matt knocks, bringing me back to myself.

"Aren't you hungry?" he asks.

"In a minute," I say.

I look at my face and now, of course, it's even worse. Red, raw, inflamed, bleeding in a couple spots. I stick pieces of toilet paper to the blood, spread out my small, selective palette of concealers and powders and shadows. I work slowly, carefully, attempting camouflage.

It still doesn't look right. I wipe it off and start again. I frown at the new bumps on my skin. The unsightly scars keep rising above the layers of makeup I apply. Why me? Why do I have to be so ugly?

Matt knocks again.

"I'm starving," he says. "Come on."

"Hold on."

"What's wrong? Talk to me."

"Nothing."

I finally emerge from the bathroom, not satisfied but at least mollified, and shake Matt, who's fallen asleep in a chair.

"Do I look okay?" I ask.

"Very nice," he says, as he always says.

We go to a fancy Asian fusion restaurant, one of those chic spots decorated with larger-than-life Buddha statues, seemingly for Western eyes and tastes. Large booths to give the illusion of privacy. Where wealthy men on business snuggle with women in dark corners, a bottle on their table. I order an exorbitantly priced cocktail while Matt sticks with beer. Our meal comes in stages, as we sink deeper and deeper into the wealth of the velvet-covered cushions. A stronger cocktail arrives decorated with a little umbrella.

"Honestly?" I say, looking around, "We could be in L.A. Or Barcelona. Or Buenos Aires. What's the point?"

"The point, my dear," Matt says, "is that we're in Delhi. The point is that today I took you to see the marble tomb erected by 20,000 artisans hired by an emperor who wanted to pay tribute to his true love."

"Would you like anything else?" the waiter asks.

I hesitate, wanting another drink.

"No," Matt says firmly. "We'll take the cheque, please."

"I was thinking of having another drink," I say when the waiter leaves.

"You don't need it, do you?" says Matt.

Not really a question.

We taxi back to the hotel in one of the old-fashioned black and yellow Delhi taxis that look like they haven't been updated since the '70s. The seats are lined with velour, and there's a Ganesha figurine dancing from the mirror.

I look longingly at the bar as we walk through the lobby.

In bed, Matt turns over and is snoring minutes later. I consider sneaking down to the bar, but think of the effort it would take. I fall asleep.

Back in Pune, Matt returns to work. Emboldened by our weekend trip and restless in the hotel, I finally leave on my own. I bring a shawl to cover my shoulders and ask the driver to take me to a Jain temple. Once there, the attendant indicates I have to remove my shoes, so I stuff them into the cubbyholes provided. At first I step hesitantly on the sparkling clean marble floors, tiptoeing, but gradually I embrace the freedom of bare feet, the refreshing coolness against my weathered soles.

I am transfixed by the elaborately bejewelled Buddhas, the incense, the bowing, the pregnant silence. A quiet devotion that is foreign to me.

I stay as long as I can, hoping to absorb some of the stillness.

That night I want to tell Matt about the temple, but he's already sleeping. The bed is so big you could fit two extra people between us, a small island swathed in white with a hill of pillows. We stay chastely on our own sides. I'm relieved, really. Lately I'd found myself turning away when Matt turned toward me in bed, pretending to be asleep. Having sex with him had come to seem like an insurmountable chore. But I'd thought things would be different, once we were away. It hasn't been long, and already I'm wondering how this trip is going to solve anything at all.

When Matt and I told friends we were going on a trip around the world, most reacted with raised eyebrows.

"What about work?" they asked.

In our thirties and childless, this wasn't what was expected of us.

"They're just jealous," Matt said of our child-rearing friends.

It had become harder and harder to schedule evenings out. Babysitters required forethought, and any attempt at spontaneity was met with a mixture of bemusement and envy.

"It's now or never," said Matt.

My parents' first question, of course, was about money.

"Oh, really?" my mother said when I admitted Matt was paying, not bothering to hide the judgement in her tone. Then she changed the subject. My father kept quiet about the whole thing, letting my mother speak for both of them.

Matt only informed his family a week before we left. "Have a nice time, dear," was the only reply he got, from his mother. "Make sure your shots are up to date."

With Matt's funds, we had enough for six months if we weren't too picky about where we stayed and didn't splurge too much on food. Matt hadn't complained when he'd had to pay rent the last few months, when I'd run out of money entirely. But there was another condition of Matt's, besides the credit card. I had to pack light. I spent days choosing what to take with me.

We had several discussions about the criteria required to make it a real "around the world" trip, but finally decided we didn't want to box ourselves in. So the plan became to make minimal plans, to go with the flow. Matt had a project to wrap up at the Pune office before taking his leave of absence, so we'd start there. We planned to go to China after a month in India. From there, we'd see how we felt. I had a sense there was something Matt was escaping, but I didn't want to think too hard about what it might be. And of course I had my own reasons. Because, really, when you go on a trip like that, you're almost always running away from something, aren't you?

When we arrive in China there is no Google, and I'm forced to go cold turkey. We hadn't planned for this. I stare at my empty browser, making a mental list of all the things I would otherwise be googling: Tiananmen Square, Mao, best noodles in Beijing, hutongs, Chinese restaurant etiquette, tipping in China, what to order at dim sum.

After India, the traffic in Beijing feels almost orderly, the streets so empty and clean. Walking around all day surrounded by slim, immaculately dressed and made-up women in insanely high heels, I feel exposed. When night falls, we go to a night market where stall after stall contains exotic food sliced and mounted on sticks. Matt eats a scorpion and I take his photo.

"It's crunchy," he says, "like crispy chicken."

He wants to take one of me. I hold the stick up to my frozen smile, unable to bring myself to eat scorpion. I nibble glazed fruit instead. I feel the sugar on my skin almost immediately, thick and cloying.

The next morning we climb the Great Wall, because that's what the guidebook says to do, and I marvel at the women who are able to navigate the wall in skirts and stiletto heels.

"It's a talent some women have," says Matt. "They can do anything in heels, like they were born in them."

It's a talent you don't have, is what I hear. Fuming, I look down at my dirty jeans, flat feet. The blue Converse sneakers felt hip at home, but stodgy and unfashionable here. Maybe I should have bought the pink ones.

Back at the hotel, I stew in my misery while Matt books discounted domestic flights for the rest of our time in China. The best word to describe Matt is *capable*. He has a facility for getting things done unlike anyone else I know. It's part of what attracted me to him. For me, getting stuff done is so much harder. I can't leave the house until my face is perfect, which, I admit, sometimes takes hours. It's much faster for Matt to run out and grab groceries or takeout. I can't make a phone call or have a conversation with a co-worker without analyzing every exchange. Better for Matt to make dinner reservations or call a taxi. Being in the world, among people, is mentally exhausting. When I'm with Matt, he takes care of the daily exchanges, thinking nothing of dealing with hotel clerks, restaurant waiters, or taxi drivers while I sit mutely beside him.

"You're getting to be too dependent on him, you know,"

my best friend Sadie said before I left. "You can't keep letting him take care of everything for you."

"Why not?" I asked.

She rolled her eyes. Sadie was single, and in the months before Matt and I left, a new strain had entered into our friendship.

"You used to be so independent," she complained. "Now you can't go anywhere without him."

"We're a couple. That's what couples do."

"Just promise me you'll take some time for yourself when you guys are travelling. Don't let him dictate everything."

A few things Sadie didn't know. Back when I was so independent, as she calls it, I'd been barely holding it together. She didn't know about the nights I got stuck in front of the mirror and didn't go out, collapsed into bed with a bottle of wine instead. She didn't know about the therapist I started seeing six months after meeting Matt. She didn't know how much better I've been since Matt. About all the little things that helped. Rituals.

A little known fact: I used to be a model. Not, I should say, the type of model you're thinking of. I'm not that type of beauty. Certainly not. No, I was a catalogue model. For department store clothing. The girl-next-door type. Sometimes they cut my head out of the shot, just used my body to model the clothes. The pressures are different when you're a commercial model, but still, there are appearances to keep up. It started slowly, a product here, a product there. Different creams for my skin, expensive creams. Too expensive even when my career was at its peak. Trying to quell the acne that sprang up when I became anxious, I started lurking around cosmetics counters, stalking the aisles of facial products. Sweeping little bottles and tubes into my purse.

Eventually, I was caught. Unluckily for me, it was at the department store where I'd been modelling. My catalogue career was over, but my addiction to beauty products only intensified. I developed rashes from all the creams, and that only led to more creams, temporary fixes.

I went for a special facial that promised smooth, acne-free skin. I endured hours of painful extractions. Peels. Afterward, my skin did look nice. A little red, but glowing. The next day, however, little bumps started sprouting, angrier and angrier. By the following day, my face looked like it was covered in barnacles.

An allergic reaction, the doctor said. The medicine she prescribed only made it worse, and I visited three dermatologists before I found something that helped and calmed my inflamed skin. After that, though, even after my skin had supposedly healed, I couldn't look in the mirror without seeing all the scars. Scars from the treatment and subsequent medication layered on top of my original acne scars. My friends told me it wasn't noticeable, but I knew they were just being kind. They wanted me to stop worrying and get on with life. I watched endless makeup tutorials, looking for the best form of camouflage. I forced myself to pay for products this time, and they added up quickly. I couldn't stop looking in the mirror, seeing what I didn't want to see. Wine helped, at night, soothing me enough for sleep.

When we leave the room again and go back out, I am surprised to find that wine bars in China do not necessarily have wine. I drink a Tsingtao beer instead, which goes better with the oppressive heat. My first time drinking a beer I actually enjoy.

"Are you sure you want to start drinking beer?" Matt asks.

I suppose Matt focuses on the alcohol because it's tangible, evidence. He can't see what goes on behind the closed bathroom door; he can't read my thoughts. Beauty products are more benign to him. He likes the way my face looks with makeup. He's told me so.

We pass through streets where women have sewing machines set up on the side of the road, portable outdoor tailors beside vendors with huge baskets of clementines. Peering down alleyways, I see evidence of domestic life, bicycles resting against brick, potted plants convening in groups, red paper lanterns. Men sit in metal folding chairs in the shadows outside shop doors, and some gather to play mahjong.

"That's the life," says Matt, watching a group of men.

"Sure, it's a life," I say.

I'd seen a documentary about the hutongs, homes made among narrow alleys and courtyards where generations of families lived communally, and how they were being destroyed to make way for more modern housing, for subway lines and high rises.

"You couldn't sit still long enough to play mahjong, anyway," I tell Matt.

In Yangshuo, we rent bikes and cycle dirt roads that wind through fields of rice paddies. There's no one around save a handful of water buffalo and a lone woman in a broad straw hat harvesting rice. I'm comforted by the loneliness of the landscape.

I stop so suddenly the bike's brakes squeak in protest. A child peers up at me from the middle of the road, all huge brown eyes, silky black hair in pigtails. She tilts her head to one side and speaks, but of course I don't understand. She comes toward me and touches my wrist. I am transfixed, heart swelling. I don't know what else to do, and am also vaguely afraid of being accused of something untoward, so I tear myself away and keep biking, trying to catch up with Matt's black T-shirt that's already receding into the distance. Her shining brown eyes stay with me. I wonder what she wanted.

"Money," says Matt.

"You think?"

"Of course."

My scalp stings from the unrelenting sun and the part in my hair, the only place I haven't applied sunscreen, is fire red. The Tsingtao beer I have back at our hippie hostel is the most refreshing thing I've ever tasted.

That night we stroll through a night market and watch a woman slicing a huge durian fruit. She holds out a piece on a knife and offers it to me. It tastes fleshier than I expect.

The first time I tried durian was when Matt and I had dinner at his friend Amy's house. She was a former classmate from his MBA days. It was early in our relationship, and I was unprepared for Amy's elegant, discreet beauty, and even more unprepared for how quickly Matt fell into the rhythm of this group, people I'd barely heard of, as they gossiped about former classmates, discussing who had gone on to do what and who was making big bucks. I watched Amy touch Matt's arm as she laughed at something he said and wondered if they'd slept together.

I sipped nervously at the white wine Amy served, gulping it down faster than I meant to. She, ever the graceful hostess, kept refilling my glass. By the time she served dessert, I was tipsy. I picked up a piece of the curious fruit she'd set out on a platter, inspecting it and bringing it up to my nose.

"Wow," I said. "Stinky."

Matt turned to me in alarm, but Amy laughed.

"Of course," she said. "It's durian. It's supposed to be stinky. Try it."

I did. It tasted disgusting.

"Yum," I said.

"You don't have to lie," Amy said. "I know it's an acquired taste. But trust me, it tastes so much better in China."

She was right. In fact, I wouldn't have guessed it was the same fruit. Matt takes a large bite. He looks lost in thought, and suddenly I need to know.

When we get back to the room I unearth a bottle of Indian whiskey I'd tucked into my suitcase.

"Care for a drink?"

"I guess," he says, sighing. "If you really want."

"Isn't Amy's family from somewhere around here?" I ask, once we're suitably equipped with plastic cups of whiskey.

"Amy?"

His feigned surprise tells me all I need to know.

"The durian," I say. "It made me think of her."

"Oh, right. I'd forgotten about that."

"Do you still think about her?"

"What do you mean, still?"

"Matt, c'mon."

"C'mon, what?"

"You can tell me! It was before we even met."

"There's nothing to tell."

He's become sullen. I retreat into my whiskey. I pour myself another, then another. I go to the bathroom and lock the door. Inside, I approach the mirror and stand so close my nose touches the glass. From here, I can see all the whiteheads brewing on my chin, all the blond hairs on my jawline. I pinch the whiteheads, one after the other, trying to release all the impurities from my face. I pluck the hairs, but there are so many it's hard to stop.

I wake up hours later, slumped on the bathroom floor. I hear Matt snoring on the other side of the door.

The next morning, we both shower and go for breakfast, drink our tea like nothing happened. Matt goes biking again. I stay behind.

Once he's gone, I pull out a postcard I found in the lobby. I run my fingers over the letters. Banyan Tree Spa. At reception, they tell me it will be a 20-minute cab ride. I agree and they arrange everything. Luckily, Matt's given me a little pocket money. I opt for their top-of-the-line facial. She starts with a back massage, but I can't relax. As she lathers on cream after cream, however, my hopes rise and my fears dissipate with each layer. I feel her slaying the dead skin cells, exfoliating, extracting. She recommends some products for continued improvement and I buy them all. This is an emergency, after all, so I pull out my secret credit card.

I tiptoe into the room, hiding the bag behind my back. Matt is sitting on the bed.

"Not again, Janice."

"What?"

"What's behind your back?"

He takes in my face, its telltale redness.

"You went for a treatment, didn't you?"

I shrug.

"How much did you spend?"

Another shrug.

"Come on, Janice. We've been over this. How did you pay for it, anyway? Your credit score is going down the tubes, you know."

"And until it does …"

He finally drops it and we reach a testy equilibrium, go into town for dinner. We eat Yangshuo beer fish, bitter melon and egg, stuffed Li river snails. It's hot. We drink beer. We don't talk much.

"Let's go to Vietnam," I say the next morning. "We're already pretty far south."

I also want to avoid Hong Kong, its Western-style shops and conveniences.

"I could go for some pho," says Matt.

"Are you really reducing a whole country, a whole culture, to a bowl of noodles?"

"We can do all the cultural stuff you want," he says. "Especially if it's free."

We fly to Hanoi and eat our way down the coast. Da Nang, Hoi An, Nha Trang, and finally Ho Chi Minh City. Matt makes sure we don't stop moving. We stay together and I have no time for spas. We take street food tours and cooking classes, walk through outdoor wet markets, spend time at the beach, ride scooters. At an indoor market full of tailors, I pick dress styles out of a catalogue, with Matt's approval, and have several made by the next day. We caffeinate on Vietnamese iced coffee, so thick, rich and sweet with condensed milk. I am delighted by the big bundles of fresh green herbs that top every dish. We are sobered and horrified at the War Remnants Museum in Ho Chi Minh and take to a bar, drink our bia hoi in silence.

"I could really go for a decent croissant," Matt says, finally.

Croissants, or even bread, have been hard to come by.

"I could go for an espresso," I say.

"Next up: France," Matt says.

"France?"

"Oh," Matt looks at me. "Will that be hard for you?"

This is the closest Matt comes to acknowledging my condition, if you can even call it that. He thinks I'm just a woman who likes to look nice. That's all. Nothing wrong with that. On good days I think he's right, but on bad days I think he's deluded, too.

I think of the vast stretch of world we'll be skipping over to fly from Hanoi to Paris. I'd imagined us heading to Cambodia or Laos after Vietnam, or maybe Japan or Bali. This feels like cheating.

We fly to Paris with visions of baguettes, croissants, stinky cheese, charcuterie, espresso and red wine bouncing around in our heads. Even the in-flight turbulence doesn't sway us. I try not to think about Paris' legendary department stores, the French perfumes, the cosmetics counters. I'll stick to bakeries and fromageries, I tell myself.

I dread those moments of anxious anticipation around the baggage carousel, and cannot suppress a big smile of relief when my easily recognizable neon pink bag pushes its way through the black rubber flaps. Matt's bag is a practical black, and we misidentify a few before finding his.

"Let's rent a car," Matt says, as we pass a car rental counter.

"Do we need a car in Paris?"

"We should get out of Paris," he says. "Paris is expensive. It's big, overwhelming, too busy."

Of course he wants to get me away from Paris.

"Do you know how much a hotel will cost in Paris, even a shitty one? Let's drive south to a smaller town. They have croissants and espresso everywhere in France," he says.

I'm disappointed. I'd imagined us drinking champagne in a Parisian wine bar, sipping espresso while discussing the contemporary art exhibit at the Centre Pompidou, breaking baguette and sipping wine from plastic cups in a park, maybe being cheesy one night and taking a bateau-mouche at sunset, adding our lock to the Pont des Arts. I had also hoped to inject some Parisian style into my travel wardrobe. But I know Matt is right about the expense.

We rent a car and make only one stop in Paris. I'm not suitably made up to enter a Parisian establishment, but there's no choice. I don't drive standard. Matt double parks and puts on the hazards while I duck into a bakery and buy two croissants and a country-style baguette. At the fromagerie next door, I pick two cheeses: one hard and sharp, the other stinky and oozing. At the cash, I grab a bottle of white wine. I'm still wearing my sundress and sandals, and even with a sweater, I shiver violently as I rush back to the car. It had been warm in Vietnam, and we hadn't thought much about the weather in France at this time of year. It's grey, a distinct chill in the air.

I hand Matt a croissant. He takes a huge, flaky bite, spewing crumbs, and we head south. As we pull away, I remember I have no corkscrew, glasses, or way to chill the wine. Matt is fiddling with the GPS, but he can't get the maps to load. He gives up and eats the croissant with one hand while he drives.

"You navigate," he says. "There's a map in the glove compartment."

Matt is the one with a sense of direction, so I'm nervous. I look at the map, trace a line with my finger, and choose Limoges. Far enough but not too far. Three and a half hours, I estimate.

"Want the other croissant?" I ask Matt.

He shakes his head, already satiated.

At my request, Matt pulls off at an *aire de repos* for an impromptu picnic. We dig through our suitcases to find extra layers. I rip off a piece of baguette and a piece of cheese, chew methodically. Exercise for my jaw after so many bowls of soft noodles in China and Vietnam. I eye the bottle of wine.

"How can we open it?" I ask Matt.

"Warm wine? Are you that desperate?"

Suitably shamed, I get back in the car.

I trace the progression of canola fields up and down hills until I'm dizzy. They're dormant at this time of year, and I'm disappointed we won't see the shock of bright yellow I've only seen in photos. We get lost after I miss a turnoff, and it takes an extra hour to reach Limoges. Matt walks ahead of me, dragging his suitcase. I trail behind, wanting to stay out of the path of his bad humour but also trying to navigate the cobblestones in the kitten heels I bought in Beijing. I let him pick the hotel, and luckily there's a vacancy at the first place we try, a small, ageing establishment just off the main square.

I need to recalibrate the situation, so after we check in, I steer us to a café and order two glasses of white wine without consulting Matt, who doesn't speak much French.

I think back to India's temples, which range from incredibly elaborate complexes with millions of visitors per year to small makeshift shrines set up in the corner of a shopping district where you can stop to pray after buying a miniskirt at H&M. I try to channel some of the stillness I felt back in that Jain temple.

"Isn't this nice?" I say, once we have our wine.

"Sure," he says absently.

I sip my wine to fill the uncomfortable silence. Matt barely touches his, so I finish it for him. It's as if he's in a dream state; he doesn't notice. At this point in our trip, we have little left to say to each other. But the wine soothes me until I am smiling up at the grey sky visible through the window.

Matt and I were set up. In retrospect, it feels too easy, the way we fell together. Like two seagulls that just happened to land on the same rock a long way from shore. Sadie's boyfriend at the time, Julian, was a good friend of Matt's. Looking back, I wonder what made Julian think Matt and I would make a good couple. Were we just the only two single people he knew? Did he and Sadie think it would be fun to double date? But Sadie never took to Matt, and she and Julian broke up six months later. He cheated on her with an intern at his office, a young man by the name of Lucas, much to Sadie's horror, although she was always quick to clarify that she wasn't homophobic.

At surface level, Matt and I didn't have much in common. He was fresh out of his MBA program and already rising in the ranks at a financial consulting firm. He liked to stay in on work nights, order Chinese, watch *The Daily Show*, read *The Economist*, get a good solid eight hours of sleep. I read only novels, still went dancing at clubs where the bass overpowered the melody and during the week could often be found out at the bar later than was strictly sensible. For some, drinking is a way to withdraw from the world, but for me, introvert that I was, drinking was a way of engaging with it, giving me the freedom to step outside the drudgery of my internal mono-logue. Interactions became smoother, less painful. I didn't let drinking interfere with my life, aside from the Advil I popped most mornings to ward off the lingering headache that was a constant ebb at the shores of my consciousness.

Matt liked hiking, I was told, which made me remember the hiking boots in a box under my bed, as pristine as the day I'd bought them. I worked in finance, so Matt and I had that in com-mon, but I was in the marketing department, and my job was just that: a job. For Matt, it was much more than that. At least, he wanted it to be. He wanted it to mean something. I didn't har-bour any such illusions about my dead-end marketing job.

We only committed to drinks for our first date (me: Hen-drick's and tonic; Matt: Hoegaarden), but drinks progressed into dinner and dessert moved on to after-dinner drinks. At midnight, a nightcap seemed in order, and so we laughed our way into a Cuban-themed bar for mojitos.

"I miss the outdoors," Matt said.

He was glowing, tipsy, looking up at the palm trees sur-rounding us.

"They're fake," I told him.

"Buzz killer."

It was only later I learned how unusual it was for him to drink so much.

For a second I worried he was actually angry—is he one of those drunks?—but he quickly resumed a facade of normalcy.

"It's just, you know, back before I was working, I used to do more stuff," he said.

"Stuff?"

"Hiking, camping, canoeing, fishing. Outside the city, where you can see the stars. Just you and … whatever's up there. Not as much bullshit in between, mediating your experience. No smartphones."

"Are you religious?"

"No! It's just, I like to get away. Be somewhere quiet, have the chance to reflect. Without the pings and blings and beeps."

"What's stopping you from doing that now, on weekends?"

He made a face, moving his lips from one side to the other. Then he went suddenly still, eyes wide.

"Let's go tomorrow," he said.

"Tomorrow?"

It was already past midnight.

"Have you ever been canoe camping?" he asked.

"No."

"You're going to love it," he said.

I was pretty sure I wasn't going to love it, but I liked him enough to go along with it.

We barely slept. A taxi dropped me off at 3 A.M. and I scurried inside to dig out my unused hiking boots. Matt picked me up a few hours later, hopped up on caffeine from the looks of the giant travel mug in the cup holder, the car loaded with camping gear and a large cooler. We headed north, where we rented a canoe and booked a campsite.

I lowered myself into the canoe and sat in the front, leaving the steering to Matt.

"Good ol' J-stroke," he said, stretching his arms with the oar held above his head before dipping it into the water.

I didn't know what that meant, but it sounded like he knew what he was doing. I paddled, trying to keep my stroke steady so Matt could follow, holding my face up to the sun. After half an hour, the water started getting choppier, the canoe swooshing upward and slapping back down against the water.

"Paddle harder," Matt told me.

After about ten minutes it became work more than pleasure. My arms were getting sore, and the water was so rough I worried we'd tip over. But we kept going. After a while I noticed the shoreline looked familiar. We'd been going in circles, stuck in a current.

"What's happening?" I asked Matt.

"Just keep paddling," he said.

Twenty minutes later, we still hadn't made progress, and my arms felt like they were about to give out.

"Maybe we should ask someone for help," I said.

"We're okay," Matt said. "Just keep going."

"No, really," I said. "I think we should go toward shore."

"Fine," Matt said tightly.

I tried to push us closer. Someone was standing in the water. A young boy in a blue-and-red striped T-shirt. I waved to him. He waded out a bit further, and as we got closer, he grabbed our canoe and pulled, walking us in until the tip hit beach.

"There's a strong current there," he told us. "Looked like you were caught in it. You have to be careful."

He looked about ten, but he sounded so authoritative.

"Thank you," I said.

Matt didn't say anything. The boy wandered off down the beach. I looked for his parents, but didn't see anyone else around.

My legs shook as I climbed out of the canoe and onto sandy shore. I didn't know Matt well enough to know how to ease the tension. He dragged the canoe further up onto the beach, stopping underneath some trees, and then came to sit beside me.

We decided to leave the canoe where it was and make our camp for the night. We pitched our tent and got in, collapsing into each other's arms, finally able to laugh at ourselves. We'd only met the day before, but were already bound by the experience. When it started to get dark, Matt built a campfire while I sat in the sand and watched. When I couldn't see his face anymore except for by the glow of the fire, he admitted he'd never steered a canoe.

"I didn't think it would be very complicated," he said. "I've been canoeing before, but one of my friends always steered."

Matt cooked steaks on a grill over the fire, seasoning them with barbecue sauce and steak spice. I sifted through his cooler, hoping for a bottle of wine, but there wasn't one. Not even beer.

I was only partially exaggerating when I told him it was the best steak I'd ever had. We climbed into our tent. The sex was awkward, but I attributed it to the lack of alcohol. I inhaled the smoky campfire smell of my hair as I fell asleep.

The next morning, I woke up early. I'd washed my face in the camouflage of dark, and now I didn't want Matt to see me without makeup. I grabbed my cosmetics bag and snuck out of the tent. The water was so still I used it as a mirror to apply my layers of product. I was on the final step, mascara, when I heard Matt behind me.

"Makeup?" he asked. "What do you need that for? We're camping."

I shrugged, unable to articulate myself.

Back in the canoe, it only took twenty minutes to reach the car.

From Limoges, we drive south all the way into Spain. I choose another town by closing my eyes and pointing at the map. We drive and drive, remaining faithful to my finger and bypassing Toulouse, Carcassonne, even Barcelona. As we get further into Spain, the road narrows and we wind our way along cliffs, through mountains and past vineyards and rivers. It gets warmer, and I'm relieved to feel the sun on my skin again. My awe increases as I stare out the window. I feel guilty that Matt has to keep his eyes on the road and its vaguely treacherous turns.

In Torroja del Priorat, tiny streams of sweat make inroads from my upper thighs all the way to my feet. In the mid-day heat, the small town seems abandoned by everyone except an occasional lazy fly or a dog curled up in a spot of shade. The dogs are sleeping so deep they don't stir as we pass.

"It's siesta time," says Matt, stopping to remove his hat and wipe his forehead.

He's gotten a tan since we've been gone, I note. It ages him but also makes him look more handsome.

"Do you think my arms have gotten smaller?" he asks, craning his neck to look at his bicep.

When Matt and I first met, he was a little pudgy, a little pale. Those years of concentrated MBA study and moving up the ranks. He'd developed an unfortunate M&M habit, he confessed. But a few years after we started dating, he looked in the mirror one day and seemed to see himself for the first time in years. Something blossomed in him that caused him to go to the gym, add "work out" to his lexicon, drink protein shakes. His body slowly hardened to his efforts until he was trim and fit. He didn't stop there. He became obsessed, his muscles growing to the point I wondered if he was taking steroids on the sly. He spent hours at the gym after work; I'd call him and beg him to come home for dinner, which got later and later. We can't keep eating at midnight, I told him. Having shed his doughier self, he walked with a new confidence. I can't say it wasn't attractive. I liked to think I'd inspired this change, but even I knew that was unlikely.

"A guy doesn't just start working out all the time when he's been with a girl for a few years," Sadie had said. "That's a new relationship thing. Or a trying to get a girl thing."

I knew what she was thinking, and I resented her for it. I wasn't about to admit to Sadie that our sex life wasn't great. I mean, the sex was actually good, when we had it. The "when" was the problem. Matt spent all his time at work or at the gym. At night, by the time I was through my bathroom routine, he was usually fast asleep.

"He's not cheating," I told Sadie.

She shrugged in a way that meant she didn't believe me but wasn't going to make a fuss.

Matt's biceps do look a little smaller, but of course I don't tell him that.

"You look great," I say, kissing him on the cheek. "Healthy."

We splurge on a nice room. It's off-season and we're the only guests, so we have a whole villa to ourselves. After several cramped hotel rooms with barely enough space to open both our suitcases, we're happy to spread out. There's a big wrap-around balcony out back with a view of the hills and vineyards. We go down there to eat breakfast the next morning: croissants, jam, fruit, cheese, coffee, mimosas with local cava. The morning warms as it pushes toward noon, and we're still sipping mimosas, reluctant to move, tired of tourism. I eye the half-empty bottle of cava, wondering if Matt will judge me if I make another.

"Maybe we should just stay here, read or whatever," I say.

"Really?" asks Matt. "You would sit here all day?"

We'd agreed, before coming on this trip, that Matt wouldn't spend any time in gyms. But I know he's been doing push-ups and sit-ups whenever I go into the bathroom, improvising chin-up bars and weights where he can, and he's been pushing us to walk as much as possible, preferably up hills, at a high speed.

"Sure, why not?" I sweep my hand to indicate the view. "It's beautiful."

I affect a calm I don't necessarily feel, partially to bait him. I can't help it.

"Why not take a walk around, work off this breakfast?"

I shrug. The sun and the cava have made me lazy.

"It's up to you," I say.

"Translation: no thank you," Matt says.

The first time we travelled together, I quickly realized I would have to adjust to his rhythm if we were going to make it work. Matt is a particularly energetic traveller, the type who checks into a hotel, sets his bag down in the room, and is im-

142

mediately ready to head out and explore. I need to ease into things, deliberate the options. And nothing makes Matt more restless than sitting around a hotel room waiting for me to deliberate the options.

"Ok, fine, let's go somewhere," I say.

We go back to the room. Although I had every intention of going somewhere, we spend the rest of the day in bed. Not having sex, of course, just lazily surfing the internet and napping. By the end of the day, I feel disgusted with myself. And with us. We're failing as around-the-world travellers. But I am so tired.

After weeks of driving, we finally reach Spain's southernmost point. We decide to head north again, back toward France. We haven't gotten very far when I spot a little speck of sunny yellow in the distance. Canola? This early? As we get closer, I see it's a field of sunflowers. They haven't yet bloomed, but here and there I see a tiny splash of yellow, the flower still closed but optimistic. Cheered by their potential for brilliance, imagining the field of sunflowers I've always wanted to see, I ask Matt to pull over. He grumbles, but does as I ask.

I stumble out of the car on stiff legs and rush into the sunflowers. When I reach the middle of the field, I turn back and look at Matt. He's leaning against the car, scowling, and, shockingly, smoking a cigarette, something I've never known him to do. Where did he get it? I motion for him to join me, but he shakes his head. I wander back toward the car.

"They'll be so pretty in a few months. I've always loved sunflowers."

"I prefer to just eat the seeds," he says.

I am overtaken by a new sense of urgency.

"I have to go to the bathroom. Do you think there's a rest stop nearby?"

"Go in the bushes. I don't want to waste more time stopping again."

"What's the rush?"

"Go in the bushes," he insists. "I don't know when we'll find the next bathroom."

Matt's stare feels like a challenge. He knows I'm prissy about this sort of thing. I grab some Kleenex from my purse and stalk off, heading for a small cluster of scrubby bushes to one side of the sunflower field. I camouflage myself as best I can, thighs poised to move quickly if I see a car coming over the hill. Mission accomplished, I step away, so swiftly I trip over a rock. *Fuck.* I stumble into a bush, and a prickly branch slices into my skin. The blood is crimson against my lily pale inner arm. Maybe it's the sun, but I feel queasy.

I grip my arm and walk back to the car.

"Come here," Matt says when he sees the blood.

He pulls a first aid kit out of the trunk, crouches beside me and swabs my arm with a disinfectant wipe that makes me wince. He applies a glob of Polysporin and a Band-Aid.

"See?" he says. "No problem."

I nod.

"But you should really be more careful."

I look up at him, annoyed. We pull back onto the highway, the car reeking of his cigarette. For the first time, I think maybe I won't stay with Matt, not until marriage. Just like that. As if the decision is something outside of myself that I can't control.

144

We've only made it partway around the world when things start falling apart. I trace our route on the map, rueing the smallness of what we've covered. Pathetic. The end of this six-month grace period, so fuzzy at the beginning of our trip, is coming into sharper focus and I guess we're both worrying about what will come after, what real life will bring. We get sloppy. We forget to eat lunch one day, breakfast the next, don't bother to book hotels in advance and waste time searching when we arrive. We pack, drive, sit, walk, eat and drink mechanically, forgetting to make the effort of real conversation.

We're in the middle of France: small, winding roads, my espresso-filled empty stomach, a reminder of the cigarette smoke clinging to my hair each time we round a curve. I feel seasick. Matt always laughs when I say that, because I'm almost never at sea but more often in a car, train, bus or plane. But seasick is how it feels to me. My eyes are burning behind my sunglasses and I'm too tired to find an elastic to tie my hair back.

In Valence we go for dinner at a nondescript local bistro, the type that litter France. The waiter suggests a glass of champagne as an *apéro* and I accept, charmed. Matt gives me a look and I know he's thinking of our dwindling finances, but I am undeterred. I want us to have a real conversation for once, to talk about what's next, and I know that a liberal dose of alcohol is the best way to facilitate that. I become more expansive when drinking, my conversational possibilities so much wider. I choose a bottle of red at random (I never could keep all the French wines straight, something that hasn't changed since being here) before even looking at the food menu, more interested in drinking than eating. Châteauneuf-du-Pape. New castle of the pope, I translate. Sounds festive. Red wine tastes like red wine to me. I know

I should be able to taste the difference, but I can't, not really. The food is slow in coming, and the bottle is half gone before it arrives. Matt hasn't even refilled his glass. He's busy with his Blackberry, checking work emails even though he's supposed to be on leave.

I focus on eating, filling my rocky stomach with cherry-soaked magret de canard.

"So, where to next?" Matt asks when our plates are empty.

I reach for the bottle. Matt gives me a look I don't like but I ignore him.

"I don't know."

The waiter suggests a digestive to go with dessert. How charming, I think, that the French drink more to help digest their food.

I'm stumbling by the time we head back to the hotel.

"It's these damn cobblestones," I tell Matt. "They're not meant for heels. What do the women wear around here, anyway?"

"Uh huh," he says.

"No, really."

"And it has nothing to do with the wine?"

Why can't he let me have a little fun?

I don't remember getting back to the room, but I do remember waking up and having to run to the bathroom. I remember the cool of the porcelain against my legs as I sat on the bathroom floor, wondering if Matt was awake listening to me puke. For once, I don't even glance at the mirror as I wash my hands and face.

When I open my eyes the next morning, there is a pounding at the back of my skull, dull but insistent. I groan. Matt is already up, sitting stoically in a chair by the window, dressed in white.

"How you feeling?" he asks.

"Not great."

"Look, Janice, I think you need to cool it with the drinking."

"Cool it? Seriously? Come on, we're on vacation."

"A six-month trip is not the same as a week in Cuba."

"C'mon, Matt, live a little."

"That's the thing. I want to live. And it'd be nice if you did, too."

He's being a little heavy-handed, I think, before I turn over and drift back to sleep. When I wake up again I'm alone, and Matt doesn't return to the room until late in the afternoon.

We're running out of time. The next morning, Matt has an announcement. Amy is getting married in Las Vegas in two weeks, and she wants him to be there.

"Two weeks?" I gasp. "Why didn't she tell you earlier?"

"Well, she did."

I absorb this.

"Do you want to be there?"

He nods, slowly.

"I wasn't sure if it mattered. But, yeah. It's important to her, you know?"

"Right."

"I mean, we've known each other for so many years."

"Years? I thought you met during your MBA."

"Oh, no. We met when we were teenagers."

"What? You never told me that!"

"Well, we've never talked much about Amy."

"I guess not. Where did you meet, then?"

Amy, as it turns out, was a teen model when she and Matt

first met. A different calibre of model than me: she'd gone on to do runway and editorial, a real fashion model. But at the time, she was fifteen and he was sixteen, and they were both on family vacations in Maine, one of those tiny towns where, aside from the beach, the main attraction was the arcade. They'd fought for the pinball machine and agreed to take turns, striking up a friendship in the process, going for long walks on the beach when they got bored of games, buying swirly cups of frozen yogurt.

"Sounds like the stuff romantic comedies are made of," I say. "A teenage boy. A model. The beach."

I feel thoroughly betrayed by this story, something that happened almost twenty years ago. I wonder if I can order a mimosa from room service.

"Nah, there's never been anything like that between us," Matt says.

He's looking away, but I raise my eyebrows anyway.

"Really?"

"Really."

Somewhat amazingly, since Matt lived in Nova Scotia and Amy lived in Oregon, they kept in touch, by letter at first and later by email. When her modelling career took off she began to travel internationally, often for months at a time.

"I tried to visit her whenever I could. Why not take the opportunity, you know? Tokyo, Bali, Berlin, Stockholm. We never met in North America; that was too boring."

And so, I gather, their friendship took on the breathless tinge of something foreign, of that bubble that protects you from real life when you're far away from home.

"But then she told me she was tired of modelling. The pressure, the constant castings, the waiting around, the loneliness,

148

the cattiness. She was getting older. She wanted a real career, something in business. She wanted to enjoy food again, to be able to feel the sun without worrying about wrinkles. I told her I was applying to do my MBA, and she decided she'd apply, too. I didn't think she'd actually get in, because she'd never been very serious about school. But she graduated near the top of our class."

"Who's she marrying?"

"Arthur. A partner at the firm where she's been working."

"Partner. So he's got money."

"Well, yeah. It's his second marriage. He left his wife three months after Amy started."

"Uh huh. So I suppose she'll quit as soon as she gets married?"

"You're not usually so judgemental," Matt says. "I like that about you."

It turns out Matt already told Amy he'd be there.

"I emailed her last night, while you were sleeping," he says. "We need to book our tickets."

It couldn't have been a pretty comparison, me passed out in bed.

I'm annoyed at the weight this event takes on in planning the rest of our trip, how it becomes our end point, our goal. It breaks our rhythm, forcing us to cross back to North America before I'm ready.

We arrive in Vegas just in time for the bachelorette party. The main event is a male review show, Thunder From Down Under.

"A strip show, you mean," I say when Matt explains this.

It doesn't seem to occur to Matt that it's odd for him to

149

attend a bachelorette party. We're threading our way from the MGM Grand to the Bellagio, from one casino to the next, underground of course because no one walks outside in Vegas, even though staying inside quadruples the travel time. Matt shrugs, exasperated. I stop to adjust my shoes, which are killing me. That afternoon I'd gone to Dress to Kill, a discount dress shop, and bought a slinky ten dollar number. Matt's eyes widened in admiration when I came out of the fitting room, which made me buy the dress, but I don't feel like myself in it. Matt bought me new shoes, too, red heels. I piled my hair on top of my head and spent hours on my makeup, until we were late and Matt yelled through the door.

We're nearing the Bellagio when Amy comes at us and catches Matt in a bear hug. I'm not prepared. Their hug lasts longer than I think it ought to, while I stand by awkwardly. Finally, they draw apart, still clasping each other's hands. Amy puts her hand on his upper arm.

"Nice pipes," she teases.

Matt blushes. Amy turns to me.

"Hi, Janice! So glad you could make it."

To my alarm, she lets go of Matt's arm and pulls me into a hug, too. Clearly she's already been imbibing. It is her bachelorette party, after all.

"Hi," I say stiffly. "Congratulations."

Pleasantries exchanged, she guides us to a table under a needless umbrella where her girlfriends are sipping cocktails.

When we get to the show, we're seated directly in front of the stage, where bulky Australian men gyrate in G-strings. Matt is the only guy in the room, but he doesn't seem to mind. I watch him and Amy from across the table. It's true that their excited glow is one of old friends catching up more than of former lovers. But when she's not looking, I see the way he looks at her.

One of the dancers jumps up on our table, pouring a glass of water on himself and pulsing underneath it. He is dangerously close to Matt's face. Matt finally looks uncomfortable, leaning as far back in his chair as he can without tipping over. Amy looks at Matt instead of the dancer, hiccupping from laughter. I flag down the waiter and order another martini.

After the show, we wander through the Las Vegas underground, see the Statue of Liberty reconstructed in Jelly Bellys, the fake canals of Venice, the starry sky that's really a ceiling. I've never gambled. I put four quarters into a slot machine and lose them all on the first go. I decide to stop there. One of Amy's friends has better luck. She wins ten dollars and pumps her fist in the air.

"Drinks are on me!" she cries with a whoop.

But of course her winnings aren't even enough to buy a single drink in Vegas. We sit under more needless umbrellas and Matt heads for the bar. He returns with cheerful drinks for him and Amy. I'm annoyed he didn't think to offer me one and go to the bar on my own, leaving the two of them under a canopy of fake palm.

Several drinks later, I finally tap Matt on the shoulder and motion with my head. He gets up reluctantly. We say our muted drunken goodbyes. I feel clumsy in my heels as we pick our way through the jungle of slot machines, the chime of coins echoing in my head.

We pause in Venice and lean against a brick wall. I slip my foot out of my shoe and rub it, watching the gondoliers, who look remarkably similar to the gondoliers in the real Venice.

"I wonder if they come here in the off season," I say.

Matt doesn't answer.

"See? Amy's not what you thought, right?"

"I didn't really think she was anything in particular."

That's only partially true.

"She's not so bad," I say.

"You're not so bad yourself," he says.

He leans toward me but then stops, like something else has caught his attention. I turn to look over my shoulder, but all I see is slot machine after slot machine, empty, gleaming, mouths agape.

"Let's gamble," he says.

I start to protest, but he's already moving, already reaching into his pocket for bills, already exchanging bills for tokens. I trail behind, limping. I'm too tired to try to follow the logic of the game. But I understand enough to know he's losing, again and again, feeding more coins into the machine with a glassy-eyed zeal I don't recognize. Finally he reaches into his wallet and comes up empty-handed.

"Damn," he says, shaking his head.

"Let's go," I say, outstretching my arm but not making contact.

We move away, not looking at each other. He stops suddenly, alongside the canal.

"What?" I ask.

He moves in and kisses me roughly, the fake brick scratching my bare legs. The suddenness of it startles me. I feel his scruff scratching away what's left of my makeup. I try to pull away and hit my head against the wall.

"Ow," I say.

He ignores this and grasps my shoulder, pinning me against the wall and kissing me again. His hot breath makes me panicky. Like I haven't been outside for days, like all the fake walls are closing in on me. All I know is that I desperately want to escape the prison that is his arms around me. Without thinking, I push him, hard.

He backs away and looks at me with more spite in his eyes than I've ever seen.

"What's it going to take to make you happy?" he says. "Maybe we should get married. Is that it? Are you jealous of Amy?"

I look up at the fake sky and start counting clouds, turning each one over in my mind like a squishy worry bead. It's a big sky, and it may be a long time before I run out of clouds. Without the novelty of Asia or the romance of Europe, back on American soil, I look at Matt and feel as empty as this desert was before it was built up into Vegas. A flat line, devoid of vegetation.

I shake my head.

"Matt, stop," I say. "You're scaring me."

Matt kicks the wall, narrowly missing my thigh. He pushes past me. I watch him walk away. He approaches one of the gondoliers and gets into a boat. I slide down against the wall as they drift away, watching the boat get smaller until they round a bend and disappear under a bridge, until Matt's out of sight.

The Eyes of the Moose

I was opening a bottle of Barbaresco, decanting it before dinner in anticipation of its unfurling layers of pleasure, its masochistic tannins that eventually reveal violets, when my phone rang.

"Robyn. It's your father."

I stopped cold when I heard his voice. My father never called.

My mother's mother. The news rendered my to-do list irrelevant.

Danny was late, as usual. He had a bag of takeout roast chicken and soggy fries under his arm when he arrived, eyes vacant. I set the table as he typed furiously into his Blackberry.

We shared the wine between us as we ate without tasting and it disappeared quickly. Danny shook the last drops from the decanter as he complained about some bastard at work who'd gone behind his back. I listened without listening.

"My grandmother died," I said, when he paused to finish his wine.

"What?"

He stared at me.

"Why didn't you tell me?"

"I'm telling you now."

Drinking wine always let me play outside the lines. Post-Barbaresco, things got messy. I reached into my hiding place at the back of the cupboard and grabbed a pack of clove cigarettes I'd bought in India the year before.

Piling on parkas and fur-lined boots, we went out onto the balcony to sit in the snow and smoke. The chill in the air began to feel softer, its bite reduced to a caress. I moved my legs back and forth restlessly, making the bottom half of a snow angel. The taste of tobacco hidden under Indian spices was familiar, but as if from some shameful, faraway place. My first cigarette had been in a mall parking lot, back when I was sixteen and dating a guy headed for reform school. I hadn't lasted more than a few puffs. Watching Danny, I saw what he must have looked like as a smoker, back in college before I knew him. The mannerisms came back to him so intuitively. It wasn't entirely unattractive.

He stubbed the red embers into the snow and put his hands on my legs to still them. Back inside, we shed our parkas and burrowed under the duvet. Sex, quick and urgent, then a deep sleep.

I flew home the next day.

Danny said he couldn't go with me, too many meetings, but I knew he was just making excuses. He always complained that my hometown didn't even have a decent sushi place.

All the flights to the Maritimes were relegated to the most remote, no-frills area of the airport, where they'd only recently installed a bar. I bounded along the moving walkway, down an empty, fluorescent-lit tunnel, my laptop bouncing uncomfortably against my thighs, my heels suddenly feeling too high.

My flight was delayed, as Maritime-bound flights always seemed to be, so I took a seat at the bar and ordered a gin and tonic. Each time I flew home I looked around the terminal expectantly, with a mixture of hope and dread, but I never saw anyone I knew anymore. I'd been away too long.

My phone jangled in my pocket.

Have a good flight, babe. Gros bisous.

The first time I brought Danny home to meet my parents, I'd had to warn him not to give my mother *la bise*. People didn't do that out east. With an anglophone father and a francophone mother, Danny had grown up with one foot in each culture, but his greetings were characteristically French. He shook my mother's hand solemnly instead.

"What do people do for fun around here?" he'd asked almost immediately after we'd set our bags down in my old room.

I took him into the backyard of the house that no longer felt like mine. We walked through a small forest to reach the swamp, a more cheerful, tranquil place than its name implied. The only sound was the whisper of the wind through the trees and the occasional call of a bird. After my mother retired, she had my father build a dock so she could observe the wildlife. Danny found this fantastically eccentric.

"Who wants to watch a swamp?" he asked. "Your mother has way too much time on her hands."

But as we lay on the dock, ignoring the ants and the mud, I began to see the charm of the place stealing over his features, softening them.

"What is that?" he asked, pointing at the sky.

It came from the interval, which is what we called the dead land beyond the swamp.

"I think it's an osprey," I said.

"Why's it going in circles?"

"Maybe it's lost?"

"Maybe something died," he said.

"I think it's only crows who do that. Or vultures," I said.

We watched as its circles got tighter, narrowing in.

"In India," I said, "the Parsis intentionally feed people to vultures."

"What? Really?"

"Yeah. It's not like it sounds. They have this thing called the Tower of Silence, and they leave their dead relatives there so that the vultures can come for them."

"That's pretty creepy," he said.

"Not to them. For them, it's tradition."

"But why?" he asked.

"It's about purification, restoring balance. They believe that when people die, evil temporarily beats out good. A dead body is unclean, and so it has to be purified. The vultures eat the flesh and the sun bleaches the bones. It can take up to a year, I read."

"And what happens to the bones after that?"

"They disintegrate. Eventually, the remains are washed out to sea."

He watched the osprey with renewed interest. It made one last especially large loop, and then it was gone.

As I sat in the front row pew the next day, the old splintered wood scratching the backs of my legs through itchy nylons,

157

I knew I should be crying, like the people around me, and I did manage a sniffle or two. But I also stared at the salt stains Montreal's unplowed sidewalks had inflicted on my knee-high black boots, regretting the three hundred dollars I'd paid for them. I thought about the chocolate bar I'd stress-eaten on the plane ride over and wondered if my inner thighs jiggled unattractively during sex.

Uncomplicated grief was too easy. Instead, a big, huge nothing bubbled up inside me, coating my throat as if to choke me. I have never been good at feeling what you're meant to feel when you're meant to feel it.

The woman in the casket didn't resemble my grandmother at all. She exuded a perfumed chemical aroma, like cherry Vicks throat drops, and her face was a pancaked orange, with an unnatural blush and eggshell-blue eye shadow. Her hair was coiffed in tight curls in a way it never had been in life.

My family formed a receiving line in the parlour as everyone shuffled out of the chapel after the service. My grandfather's tie was askew, and I moved to him to straighten it.

"I don't know who will do that now," he said. "Your grandmother always tied my tie for me."

My grandfather only had use of one arm. The other hung limp at his side. He'd refused to go to the doctor when he'd begun to lose feeling in it a few years earlier, claiming the doctor never told him anything he didn't already know. First he couldn't manage the top button of his shirt, later the button on his pants eluded him and he had to switch to Velcro, and finally his arm stopped working entirely.

The visitors streamed in before I could think of a reply, and I moved back to my place in line beside my brother, Adam.

"I'm so sorry, Margaret," a great-aunt said to my mother.

"And who's this young lady?" she asked when she came to me.

"I'm Margaret's daughter."

"Oh, I didn't know Margaret had a daughter!"

"You've been away, right dear? Where is it you live?" asked another great-aunt.

"Montreal."

They patted my brother on the shoulder and moved on.

"So, you have your eye on this one?" asked a friend of my father's, gesturing toward Adam.

"No, I'm his sister," I stammered.

He wasn't the only one to assume I was Adam's girlfriend. I rearranged our order, inserting myself between our parents, like a misshapen puzzle piece trying to fit back into the picture.

At my grandparents' house, an assortment of great-aunts and cousins I barely knew carved meat and peeled the plastic wrap off casserole dishes. They set out cold cuts, glistening cubes of unnaturally orange cheese, sticks of raw veggies, chunks of melon and pineapple, and finally a variety of sugar-laced, gooey squares. My mother put on coffee—decaf, the only kind my grandparents ever kept in the house. After a while, I slipped downstairs.

My grandfather was sitting on the couch, alone, oblivious to the bustle upstairs. For the first time in my life, he looked absolutely bewildered. He seemed to have shrunk, right there on the couch, his suit growing around him and engulfing him.

The basement, my grandfather's lair, had always frightened me as a kid. A startled deer stared out from one wall, and a jackalope (which, until my mother corrected me when I was about twelve, I believed to be a real animal) graced another. But the real king of the room was the giant moose who presided from the back wall, his glassy brown eyes fixed dreamily on some unknown point in the distance, brimming with unexpressed emotion. There was something crusty in the corner of his eye, the beginning of a tear that had hardened before it was fully formed. Those eyes had always terrified me with their constant gaze. But as I looked from my grandfather to the old moose, I found the eyes stripped of their former power. They simply looked sad, the moose resigned to its fate.

When I was growing up, men congregated in the basement to play pool or darts and drink beer, occasionally pressing a button on the jukebox in the corner, which after a series of ancient-sounding clicks, emitted mostly Elvis. It smelled different down there: musty beer, sweat, my grandfather's pomade. The women stayed upstairs in the kitchen, sipping decaf and eating cinnamon buns. Except for special occasions when my grandmother called the men upstairs for a midnight supper of lobster or clam chowder with potato scallop and chow chow, the men and women didn't mingle much. I used to try to slip downstairs to visit the men, but my mother always caught me. It wasn't appropriate for me to be down there, was all she would say when I protested.

The deep freeze had been my grandmother's only excuse for a foray into the basement. She came down every so often to get frozen fish or meat for dinner, or another bottle of her raspberry jam, a confection of legendary status in our family. My grandmother's hands had been unsteady for as long as I could remember—most noticeably each time she slid another cigarette out of a pack, held it to her lips, and struck a match—and each jar was painstakingly labelled in her shaky handwriting. It had taken cancer to convince her to flush her cigarettes down the toilet, though sometimes the house had smelled suspiciously air-freshened.

My grandmother and I used to pick raspberries from the prickly bushes in the backyard and cart them into the kitchen. We'd mash the berries until our fingers were stained bright red and brought the mixture to a rolling boil, adding piles of sugar. I'd stick my hand into the sugar when my grandmother wasn't looking and let it run through my fingers like sand. After her diagnosis, I asked for her raspberry jam recipe. She cut out the back of the Certo box and gave it to me.

Unless we were making jam, I'd preferred to be out in the backyard. There was a magic to the forest back there. It contained fiddleheads, supposedly edible although we never ate them; touch-me-nots, those strange plants whose leaves sprang inward when touched; and even a lady's slipper once. A true-blue endangered species. I loved to touch the touch-me-nots and uncurl the fiddleheads, but I didn't dare approach the lady's slipper.

Behind the forest was the swamp, and behind that was land, a vast swath of it, unoccupied until it became the river. The interval. Yearly spring floods washed out any attempt to breed life, the swamp expanding and the river creeping up the bank (some years the two met). In the interim, there wasn't much that could be done with the land. My grandfather and his friend Harry liked to pile some guns and a two-four of beer into his pickup truck and drive around down there. They sometimes hunted birds, fox, or any other animals they found, which wasn't strictly legal.

My mother had always nagged him about this habit. She

didn't believe in guns. More importantly, she worried someone she knew would see him. One night when I was twelve, gunshots pierced the darkness, closer to home than usual. After the truck pulled in, my mother marched over to accost my grandfather. She found beer on his breath.

"What if one of your grandchildren had been out in those woods?" she asked.

"Then I'd have asked where their mother was," he said.

My mother made good on a promise not to speak to him for a few months. I didn't see much of my grandfather during that time, despite the fact that he lived down the road. But my mother's resolve weakened as he got older and frailer. After his stroke, he had to get Harry to drive his truck down to the interval. He balanced the gun on his shoulder and propped it up with his good hand.

My grandparents had been married for seventy years. The night before, once we were most of the way through a bottle of wine, my mother said that watching her father watch her mother die had been the hardest thing she'd done in her life. I'd never heard her express herself so openly, so honestly. I wished she'd drink more and let all the resentment come gushing out. But she caught herself, sobered up. She said I was lucky not to have been there. I didn't feel lucky.

I sank into the couch beside my grandfather. I didn't know what to say, so I didn't say anything. After a few minutes, he took my hand. I looked over at him. The silent tears streaming down his face finally brought my own.

Late that night, I got into my mother's ageing Chevrolet and drove in aimless circles around the cluster of streets that passed for a downtown. I finally parked in a lonely spot by the river. It was snowing, the flakes heavy and moist, silent, and as I walked the deserted streets I felt the city was taking a collective breath. I'd never missed it after I left and felt guilty when others spoke of homesickness. I must be missing a gene somewhere, because that particular brand of nostalgia had always eluded me.

I went into a small pub with Irish clovers spray-painted on the windows, one of the few places open. Fiddle music rose over the din of beer-guzzling students. I sat at the bar and ordered a pint of local blueberry beer, a blond with a smattering of tiny blueberries floating in it.

"Hey."

I looked up into piercing green eyes. His eyes were the brightest spot on his face, as if they had been hand-tinted on a black-and-white photo for one of those cheesy greeting cards.

"Do I know you?" I asked.

"Nope."

He grinned, looking at me frankly. His wiry hair and dark stubble was out of place against his pale, delicate skin. And those eyes. His face a contradiction.

"But you looked kinda lost," he said.

He sat down beside me.

"You're not from here, are you?" he said.

"Yes, I am. Originally."

"Yeah, but not anymore, right?"

"I don't live here."

"I didn't think so."

"And you?"

"I'm not originally from here, but now I'm from here, if you know what I mean."

"Right."

He scoffed at my blueberry beer and ordered a Pilsner.

"So, what's your name?" I asked.

He turned to me, offering his hand in mock seriousness.

"Nice to meet you, Robyn. I'm Oliver."

"You know my name."

"A little birdie told me."

"Is this town that small?"

He pointed to my keys, which I'd left sitting on the bar. The last time Danny had gone away for business, he'd brought back a keychain with my name inscribed in gold. Half gift, half joke.

I blushed. We sipped our beer in silence.

"My grandmother died," I blurted out. "That's why I'm here, I mean."

"I'm sorry."

"Thanks."

It seemed like a funny thing to thank someone for.

"I guess that's one of the few things that brings someone like you home again. Death."

"There haven't been any births in my family lately."

Eventually, I let him buy me a second pint. Oliver wasn't someone who needed explanations. Instead, he offered information.

"I moved here for a girlfriend," he said, "but she left."

"Where'd she go?"

"Out west. She wanted to start a business—a café or a restaurant, or maybe a bookstore, she wasn't sure—and she didn't think she could do that here."

"You didn't consider going with her?"

"Nah. There's nothing for me out west," he said. "Besides, I wanted kids, but she didn't."

"Really? Usually it's the other way around."

"Hey, that's kind of sexist," he said.

"Not really. Just an observation."

"She had this whole thing about how she couldn't be responsible for a human life. She didn't think she'd done a good enough job with her own."

"That's intense."

Danny didn't want kids either. He thought we should focus on our careers. I never thought that would matter to me, but once the words had escaped his mouth and taken on a solid form, I'd felt an emptiness lodge itself in the pit of my stomach. It had been growing ever since.

The bartender dimmed the lights as we were finishing our third beer.

"Guess that's our cue," said Oliver.

I stumbled as I climbed off the barstool. Oliver's touch was warm as he caught me by the arm.

Back outside, it was still snowing. A rowdy line-up snaked outside the pizza place that I remembered as a donair shop. Without talking, we walked toward the river. The air now had that mildness of a light snowfall, and I appreciated the coolness of it. I tilted my face toward the sky and let the flakes fall on my closed eyelids. Each flake melted immediately.

Oliver must have taken this as an invitation. Although I hadn't meant it that way, I didn't stop him when he kissed me. He had a sweet, faintly musty smell. Falling into his embrace was easy, comfortable if not exactly arousing. I felt his tongue exploring my mouth, observing this sensation without thinking about whether this was something I wanted. It was already happening, after all. Things had a tendency to happen before my thoughts could catch up.

Danny would say I was being passive, one of his favourite words to describe me, along with reserved. *You overthink things*, he constantly told me. Gradually, over the five years we'd been together, I had allowed Danny's opinion to become the architect of my new self, or at least the new self I imagined constructing for myself. Seeing my family through his eyes made them look almost comically reserved and repressed, so worried they were about saying the right thing and *what others might think*, and this gave me something to define myself against, something to attempt to distance myself from. In Danny's family, no one left anything unsaid. Dinners were boisterous, loud affairs, with everyone talking over each other and multiple conversations criss-crossing the table like an intricate game of cat's cradle. He found my family cold, everyone so filtered and silently resentful. If I was unhappy about something, Danny told me, I had to speak up.

I broke away from Oliver.

"I can't," I said. "I'm sorry."

Oliver nodded. We kept walking. We walked for what felt like a very long time, crossing the train bridge that had been turned into a pedestrian bridge and doubling back, retracing our steps. Oliver talked softly about his family, his gentle sister and his delinquent brother. His sister had a daughter whose father had taken off early on, and so Oliver did his best to be a father figure for her.

He didn't try to kiss me again. Finally, we sat on the steps of the lighthouse in companionable silence, facing the river and the first signs of dawn. The river had begun to unthaw, and it lapped quietly at the shore, the lights from the bridge glinting off the water but fading as daylight rose.

"Time for coffee?" he finally asked.

I laughed.

"Yes, coffee time."

Even then I knew I'd never see him again. After we drank our Tim Horton's, I cleared the soggy snow off my mother's Chevrolet and drove away.

I visited my grandfather one last time before my flight home. He was sitting at the kitchen table when I arrived, photos and documents spread around him.

"Your mother says I should write some thank-you cards," he said.

I hadn't known that a funeral was an occasion that necessitated thank-you cards. The practicality of it pained me.

"I think you can take some time before you worry about that kind of thing," I said.

"All the same, best to get it over with."

I peeked into the bedroom on my way back from the bathroom. My grandmother's things were still there, her slip laid out on a chair, her brush full of auburn hair, the container for her teeth on the bedside table, her collection of brooches on the dresser. He was holding on for as long as he could. But now there was a sleeping bag on top of the bed.

"It saves me doing laundry," my grandfather said.

He had been watching me. I looked away, not wanting him to see the pity clouding my eyes. I glanced toward the basement. Feeling the moose's gaze seeping up the thickly carpeted stairs, I was childishly glad that I didn't have to go back down there. I sat down at the table and wrote a few thank-you cards. They were white with embossed gold lettering. It felt disturbingly final.

When I got up to leave, my grandfather gave me a one-armed hug.

"Come back soon," he said.

Danny was waiting at the airport. I saw him through the car window, with his scruffy black beard and ruffled hair I'd found so boyishly attractive, his head bent over his Blackberry. Would he leave my dresses in the closet, my purple toothbrush in the holder, keep my auburn-threaded brush after I was gone?

I kept walking, pulling my suitcase along behind me.

Out Taming Horses

A sudden dearth of pomegranates is messing with my salad plans. I call Renee, tell her I'm not sure I can make it to dinner.

"You're coming," Renee says. "Use dried cranberries instead."

Renee is a pharmacist, used to doling out orders disguised as advice.

I'm an hour late, everyone already perched around Renee's expertly-styled Moroccan print living room sipping Lillet. Renee and her husband have rules about shoe removal, a middle stair that acts as a boundary. Deprived of my knee-high boots, my otherwise demure outfit is now marred by the red and pink-striped socks my mother mailed me for Valentine's Day. Seeing them and knowing their origin, Renee rolls her eyes.

I sit on the arm of the sofa next to Renee and stuff my feet under it. Four other women in the room, and they're all wearing heels. They, I suppose, knew enough to bring a pair of indoor shoes to change into. Why didn't Renee tell me? The men, I notice, are in black socks, save one man in the corner wearing loafers.

I dangle on the edge of the conversation like an unruly bit of punctuation until a woman named Susan turns and envelops me in a spray of words.

"Have you tried going online?"

She's heard great things about eHarmony, the quality of people you can find on there. She doesn't bother to lower her voice. Renee's friends aren't the type to know many single women.

"Your profile photo will stand out with that hair," she insists.

I escape to the bathroom. *You are not equipped for this life*, I tell my reflection. Mirrors don't lie, but they don't answer, either. My red hair like a flame in Renee's otherwise spa-white bathroom. My too-pale skin lends my reflection a transparency, as if, if I stood there long enough, I might fade away. I find a bottle of mouthwash under the sink and take a swig, bring myself back to my body by focusing on the sting of menthol on gums.

I flinch when I hear the name of the man attached to Renee's arm. Trey. The loafers. I expect an upper crust financial advisor, someone with a booming voice under which yours can only slide submissively. An expense account, a doting wife who bestows expertly coordinated ties on birthdays. But the voice that accompanies the name is surprisingly soft, sonorous and soothing.

"You're Renee's sister," he says.

How to respond except to affirm?

He wears dark-rimmed glasses. Once upon a time, that was a clue. Now, who knows? A lawyer, an accountant, an artist, or, god forbid, someone "in marketing." Better not to ask. A stiff wave of blond hair that looks like it belongs in a '50s sitcom.

"I like your socks," he says.

I make a mental note to buy hordes of black socks the next time I take the bus downtown.

My therapist says I need to look people in the eye and so I force myself to look up at him. This proves uncomfortable after a second or two. That's when I notice his hand. Or, rather, his lack of a hand. Long sleeves provide some camouflage, but the bottom part of his left sleeve is clearly unfulfilled. I avert my eyes back down to my socks, not wanting to stare.

"So, Renee's sister, what do you do?"

"I …"

Renee calls everyone into the dining room. Susan clutches my arm and propels me to a seat at the end of the table. Not who I would have chosen as a seatmate, but at least she delivers me from a stalled conversation with Trey. Soon, though, I am trapped by stories of Susan's cat, Hazelnut, who has to be taken to a naturopath and given special homeopathic pills so he'll calm down and sleep. She only got the cat for her son, she confides. He's an only child and she wants him to get used to caring for others.

If there's anything more boring than people who go on and on about their kids, it's those who go on and on about their pets. Especially cats. At least dogs have personalities.

I make it through dinner with some serious fingernail inspecting. My salad lacks the crunch the pomegranates would have provided, the cranberries too artificially sweet. Renee's chicken tastes like I imagine a dog's plastic chew toy would.

I notice Trey's ring, gleaming under the light from the chandelier as he clutches the stem of his wine glass. A wedding ring, but it's on his right hand. He uses his fork to carve his chicken into manageable bites. His eyes meet mine and I feel his gaze dart through me until I look down. He's attractive—I give Renee that much.

He offers to drive me home. Renee must have put him up to it; she's an expert at convincing people to do as she likes while letting them believe it was their idea. He drives one of those fancy hybrid cars whose eerie silence creeps me out. If you listen carefully, it emits a faint purr. The familiar roar of a traditional motor is comforting, sleep inducing, and now its absence underlines our awkward silence. I'm still trying to think of something to ask him when he stops the car in front of my building and turns to face me.

I reach out, but his hand isn't there to meet mine. This happens a lot and I usually insist, frustrated by a world made for the right-handed. But this time, my hand meets an empty sleeve. Of course. He conceals it well.

He looks at my hand, which by now has dropped back down to my side. He leans in so far I think he's going to kiss me.

"Do you want to see?" he asks instead.

"No!"

I continue shaking my head until I nod goodbye as I trip out of the car and scurry into my building. I didn't even thank him for the ride, I realize when I'm already in the elevator.

Once in the safety of my apartment, I am consumed by shame. The more I try not to think about Trey's missing hand, the more I become fixated on it. I wasn't repulsed, exactly, just startled, unprepared. Why did I think he was going to kiss me?

I used to be married, too. Marriage, I learned, is not a permanent state, is not nearly as solid an entity as it first appears.

I've been trying not to think so much. My meditation teacher used to tell me the mind is like a wild horse, and I had to learn to tame mine. This teacher took an especially strict approach when it came to disciplining the mind. Some found his teachings too secular, too detached from their spiritual origins, but for me, they worked. My mind requires discipline.

Jared and I met my first morning at the centre, after I woke in a panic to the sound of a long, ominous gong at 5:30 A.M. Where was I? A small, dark room, the outline of a cot taking shape around me. The swish of bells coming down the hall.

Jared was the only person in the meditation hall when I arrived, less than five minutes after the gong. The others, I later found out, took their time washing and waking up first. I didn't know whether to say anything, whether that would interrupt his mental state. Was it fragile, the pre-meditation psyche?

We both kept silent, and soon the room filled, everyone quietly placing their cushions on the floor. I opened my eyes to peek over at Jared, even though I was supposed to be focusing inward. A mask came over his face when he was deep in concentration, the only time he looked inaccessible.

I was assigned to Jared's chore group, and we ended up in the kitchen together peeling carrots and potatoes. Not everyone was friendly toward newbies, but he was.

"The trick is to communicate with the *essence* of the carrot before you peel it," he said.

I looked at him.

"I'm messing with you."

He grinned, tossing a few carrot peels at me.

Jared had pale skin, tight blond curls. Of Irish origin, he grew up in Vancouver, where people made fun of his ghostly complexion, his scrawny appendages, his delicate nature. People there were more rugged, solid, more Mountain Equipment Co-op.

Things were easier at the centre: a strict schedule, an enforced vegan diet, few decisions to make other than whether I wanted chamomile or raspberry leaf tea. Whether to use a mantra during meditation. Most aspects of life were controlled. I became accustomed to the gongs, the ebb and flow of the centre, the people who came and went. The few who stayed.

It wasn't Jared's first meditation centre; he'd been moving through them since he was 18. I was shocked to find out he was 13 years older than me. His face didn't show it. Maybe because he'd never had to adhere to the hard lines of a 9 to 5, his face untouched by the stresses of bosses, office politics, deadlines. He brought a calm, quiet concentration to everything he did.

The only time we left the centre was to go for hikes in the mountains. We'd go in small groups, normally, but one day Jared and I went alone. We stood at the top of the mountain, out of breath, my face red. We weren't looking at each other, but at the valley below. A rare moment of perspective, a flood of thoughts and feelings. The sound of the wind rushing past my ears, amplified, like the mute button that suddenly unmutes itself.

"You've never tried to kiss me," I said.

"You've never tried to kiss *me*," he said.

Jared and I had been going to our separate cots every night, after the day spent meditating and working side by side. All our energy going into manual labour, the good of the group. Like all the individual desire had been stripped out of us.

"Can I kiss you now?" I asked.

174

It didn't live up to the setting. But are first kisses ever spectacular, if we're honest with ourselves?

We had to teach our bodies to desire again, after all that stillness had been drilled into them. Maybe we were too devout. But we were also fast learners, and before too long we were sneaking around, learning to be with our desire.

I'd planned to stay for six months, at least, the amount of time I figured I needed to really grasp the concept of meditation. But when I turned 33, one month in, I thought about how I'd never owned a couch, never signed a lease, never had a bathroom that wasn't shared. I'd spent the decade following college living in glorified dorm rooms, teaching ESL at schools across Asia. I never made a lot of money, and what I did make I spent on travel, so I lived simply in my furnished rooms. My daily bowl of ramen noodles like a meditation, I otherwise subsisted on green tea, water, dried fruit and nuts.

Jared convinced me it was time to reenter the world, that we'd go together, that he'd help me through the transformation. We'd keep up our practice, but also make a life, finally be able to have possessions. We married in a simple ceremony, our last at the centre.

I was excited about things, about amassing collections that could be grouped into decorative little piles. We moved into an empty apartment with white walls, two large backpacks our only furniture. I bought a stack of decorating magazines on credit. I sat on the hardwood floor leaning against my backpack, sipping tea and turning pages, looking at the rich colourful spreads of fabrics and textures and objects. Phrases like peach palette, salvaged materials, natural elements, weathered patina.

We didn't have any money. How to start a life like that?

Our landlord was the cousin of our friend Bernie from the centre and we'd still had to talk our way into it, get someone else to vouch for us in case Bernie had been hoodwinked (the landlord's word) by us. He was suspicious, called us hippies, but he grudgingly gave us the apartment.

It felt like a bad start. But together, Jared and I would make it work. I finagled a job at an interiors store where I could continue to surround myself with the language from those magazines. I think the owner wanted a Buddhist around to impress the customers. I didn't bother to correct her assumption. I'd been at a meditation centre, yes, but I wasn't a Buddhist. Something about westerners calling themselves capital-B Buddhists always felt false to me, a whiff of cultural appropriation. She wanted me to teach her to meditate. "Let's take a moment," she'd say, when the store was empty. She seemed disappointed when I told her to focus on her breathing. But she smiled and nodded, maybe figuring she had to be patient and earn my trust before I'd reveal more.

Other times, she treated me like an oracle, as if I possessed an internal wisdom about which arrangement of throw pillows would sell a fainting couch. I showed fabric samples, organized displays of napkin rings and dishes, arranged fake flowers in vases. I began sneaking things home, one small, meaningless item at a time, until the accumulation amounted to something bigger and, under my curatorial thumb, our apartment slowly began to resemble one of my magazine spreads. Maybe I would become an interior designer.

I fell away from the principles I'd cultivated, unconsciously in Asia and then consciously at the centre. I imbibed to the point of heedlessness. After living so simply for so long, I drank it all in,

I got greedy. I got a taste of meat and then gorged on it, craved it, started sweating upon sight of the meat hanging in the window at the butcher's shop. I told myself this was what my body needed, that these cravings were the result of an underlying nutritional deficiency. Gradually, I stopped finding time to meditate. Jared, on the other hand, kept up his practice. I went out. Jared stayed home. I made new friends, people who knew nothing about meditation. Jared's social circle didn't extend beyond the local centre, people like those he'd always known, except here they carried on urban lives, meeting only on weekends.

Without the confines of the centre and its strict rules, life became loose, woolly. I'm not sure if I was ever truly meditating. Maybe I never did it right. I never learned to accept my thoughts for what they were (always unruly, always messy) and observe them without judgement. At the centre I wanted something clean, something simple, a mind like Jared's. But the little asshole voice in my head wouldn't shut up. Back in the world, I began to see the charm of freedom in chaos.

Jared got a little dog, some poodle type thing, and named it Sharpie. I looked at the container of pens and markers on his desk and was disappointed in his lack of imagination. But at least he hadn't named it Bodhi or Sharma or Om or Shanti.

There was this thing Sharpie did. When Jared and I were in bed, he'd jump up, stick his nose at the edge of the covers until they lifted, then burrow himself in, deep down between the two of us at the foot of the bed. He was comfortable there, sheltered from the world, as we all were. I was afraid he would suffocate, but he never did.

I came home one day when Jared was still at the new centre, out taming horses, and Sharpie got down on his front paws and growled at me. Without Jared as buffer, Sharpie saw me for who I really was, and there was no affection in his approach. Jared may not have judged me, at least not outwardly, for he was a gentle, accepting soul, but his dog did. I started to feel Sharpie's eyes following me around the apartment.

Our marriage, wrecked: my fault. He was chaos in bodily form: ten years younger than Jared, a set of biceps with a tattoo of a Celtic knot, a stream of frenetic chatter. He was a warm body. He didn't care about my steak, my glass of red wine. He didn't expect me to sit in meditation for an hour each morning, to still my mind, to observe my passing thoughts with compassion. He, surely, would let the horses run free.

He was there for a night and then he was gone. But it might as well have been forever.

The next day is a new day. A blank slate, free of obsessive thoughts. I wake to streaming sunlight and keep my mind empty. I try to meditate but give up when my phone buzzes. Another friend uploading another baby photo to Facebook. All these photos, their cries for likes. Baby photos leave me cold. Suddenly my mind is not empty at all.

I'm craving things that are wholesome, or at least supposed to be, and so I make oatmeal. I peel apples for applesauce. I spray Windex and wipe all the mirrors and windows and glass tables in the apartment until they squeak. I mop the floor, which doesn't take long because my new apartment is small, barely qualifying as a one-bedroom. It's the first time I've lived alone, the first place I've had to myself. The windows are single pane and I hear every noise that passes on the street, every conversation that takes place on the sidewalk below. Friday and Saturday nights the bar next door and its cheap pints spill onto the street. I envy those students, the freedom they have, lives still in bloom. I miss the click of Sharpie's nails against hardwood.

I stopped reading the self-help books weeks ago. They sit in a small, guilty pile on the coffee table in front of the TV, stacked as if to pounce. Titles range from *Awaken the Spirit Within* to *How to Completely Change Your Life in Thirty Seconds* to *The Universe Doesn't Give A Flying Fuck About You* to the more mundane *The Life-Changing Magic of Tidying Up.* For a week after I moved in I'd sat on the couch and read them, one after the other. Now all their wisdom jumbles together. Would tidying my kitchen drawers reawaken my spirit? I've always been a neat freak trapped in a messy person's body. Jared used to say that was the root cause of my perpetual anxiety.

My phone is ringing. Renee. Renee calls a lot, the only one who calls, whether out of boredom or concern, I'm not sure. I picture Renee in the pharmacy, her shiny black hair pulled back in a smooth bun. I don't pick up. I often don't. I've always been jealous of Renee's hair, even though Renee says she'd love to be a natural redhead like me. More like orange, though, and who wants hair the colour of a carrot?

I take a deep breath, trying to reach a familiar place of stillness. I find it, just for a second.

My phone sings again and finally I pick up. Renee wants to talk about Trey. She wants me to see him. But the ring?

"Trey moved here from New York, in the fall of 2001," Renee says. I barely have time to absorb the place and date when she continues. "His wife was in one of the towers."

"I keep telling him to stop wearing the ring," Renee says. "It's time."

I wince at her offhand manner. Renee can be crass. She's not uncaring but prefers to get to the point. She doesn't believe in couching niceties. She's trained to get to the root of the problem as quickly as possible; there are always other customers waiting in line. Trey, I suppose, was once one of those customers.

"I just want you to know what you're getting yourself into," Renee says, "after what you've been through."

It's kind of her to put it that way, really, as if I'd *been through* something. In fact I feel as though I've simply slid past something.

She doesn't mention his arm, and I don't ask.

"I'd go out with him in a heartbeat, if I were single," Renee says.

This doesn't sound like a good idea.

But when it's Trey who rings, I pick up immediately. He sounds nervous, asking me to dinner. I'm surprised he called at all, given the way I bolted from the car. The place he suggests is fancy, the kind of place where the waiter wipes imaginary crumbs and changes the cutlery between courses. A far cry from the bohemian bring-your-own-wine Indian and Vietnamese places Jared and I had favoured. I worry about what Trey and I will talk about. I'm not a person who should be going on dates. And yet, why can't I let a guy take me to a fancy restaurant? Don't I deserve nice things?

When Trey arrives to pick me up, he rings the bell and then waits in the car. That same quiet car, the same long sleeves. All that training the mind, and look where I am. Back at square one. Obsessive thoughts. I wonder if he feels any sensation where his hand should be.

At the restaurant, he pulls out my chair. I reach down to

fix my sock inside my boot and knock a knife off the table in the process. A waiter hurries over to replace it.

I can't decide if alcohol would be a good or a bad idea. Trey orders a bottle, making the decision for me. Men who order without consulting? Take charge can be nice, but also gross. He looks nervous so I decide he's nice, not gross.

I know Renee will want every detail, so I try to pay attention. But halfway through dinner all I can think about is whether he'll kiss me at the end of the night, in his car, at my front door, inside my apartment, and whether I'll kiss him back. He orders fish, breaking off pieces with his fork. I'm disappointed—I would have liked to see how he would manage a steak. I find out later he uses an instrument called a knork, but only in the comfort of his own home.

"You're quiet," he says.

Normally I hate it when people say this. But he says it so quietly it sounds approving.

"So are you," I say.

"Yes," he says. "I like quiet."

He tries to ask what I do and I wave the question away. An article I read recently said the more polite question is "What's been keeping you busy?" Apparently Trey hadn't read this article. I rack my mind for a topic of conversation and come up with: dogs. Maybe I'm missing Sharpie after all. Trey says he's never liked dogs. Too much work, too much mess. Besides, he doesn't believe in domesticated animals. Animals should run free.

"But my wife wanted a dog," Trey says.

Renee warned me but I can't help myself and anyway, he's brought it up. So I ask about her. His eyes soften when he says her name, Mindy. But he continues to meet my gaze.

181

"She once told me," he says, "that if for any reason she ever went first, I had to continue on without her, that I had to find someone else. Someone quiet and tidy like me. She was a very messy person. She cooked elaborate, sporadic meals while listening to Guns N' Roses and dirtying every pot in the house."

Trey catches me looking again and we finally come around to the subject of his arm. It happened fourteen years ago, when he was 30. He was on a near-deserted island in Greece, a location his wife deemed romantic and he considered inconvenient. They were climbing down a large cliff to get to a black sand beach they'd seen from the road. He slipped, and the picnic basket, which contained not only their lunch but also two bottles of wine, three ice packs, and some rocks to secure the picnic blanket against the wind, fell on his arm. Hard.

It was nothing, at first. A bruise. But it bloomed, and the next day his hand was so swollen and green it resembled one of the Greek olives they'd been gorging themselves on. No hospital on their tiny island, and no ferries until the following day. By the time they made it back to Athens it was too late. The doctors said there was nothing they could do to save the hand.

He was tired of the stares, and his therapist suggested he be direct.

"That didn't seem to work with you," he says. "So I had to try again."

He could get a prosthetic, but really, who would he be wearing it for? It wouldn't help him, only others. His fellow subway riders, restaurant diners, coffee drinkers.

"I've reached an age where I don't care about making other people more comfortable," he says.

He orders tea and touches my hand, eyes still soft from talking about his wife. Feeling the need to confess in return, I tell him about my husband, though not about why he left. I tell him about the self-help books and how they're not helping at all.

"Did you love each other?" he asks, referring back, of course, to my husband.

I pause. Surely there was a time when we did. But by the end, we didn't. What qualifies as love? There must have been a single second, somewhere, when we crossed that line, the line that divides love from its opposite. And then another when we crossed back over.

"There were definitely moments," I say. "Perfect moments, even."

"I guess that's all we can hope for," he says. "A few perfect moments."

I smile at him and he blushes, seemingly recognizing his platitude. I shrug, signalling that I, too, sometimes take comfort in platitudes.

"Your sister described you as someone who is uncomfortable in her own skin," he says. "But I disagree."

It's my turn to blush.

"I'm working on it," I say, slowly.

"On what?"

"Acceptance."

"Me, too," he says, raising his left arm. "Me, too."

I think about my salad. Maybe the cranberries weren't so bad after all. Maybe the cranberries—aged, sweeter, less tart—were just what I needed.

How to Be a Widow

When Carrie looks up at her, pale green eyes pleading, and asks when daddy is coming home, Kelly knows she has to tell Carrie the truth. But she can soften it. Instead of saying, your daddy blew his brains out in that cabin I didn't know about until three years into our marriage, she can say: your father had a sickness in his brain, and then he died. That's what the literature recommends.

When Carrie runs up to her that first morning on the beach, at the Mexican resort where Kelly has brought her to get away from the looks, of pity, yes, but also curiosity and something a little like blame, when Carrie shows her a jagged piece of seashell and clutches it to her ear, saying she doesn't hear anything, Kelly tells her to keep listening. Carrie skips toward the water, lithe in her lavender bikini, an impulse purchase.

How to tell her more of the truth? Kelly still hasn't managed it. She wanted to talk to her on the plane, but Carrie had huge headphones clamped over her sleek little head, green eyes transfixed by the screen, and Kelly couldn't bear to break that spell. She offered Carrie a box of chocolate-covered almonds instead. Carrie eyed her suspiciously—sugar was outlawed in their house—and shook her head.

When their room is finally ready, Kelly tries not to cringe when she sees the rose petals fluttered into the bathtub, the towel swans necking on the bed, the champagne frosting in the minibar. She realizes resorts are meant for couples. Carrie jumps onto the bed and decapitates the swans with a swift kick of her flip-flop-clad foot.

Kelly's mother had suggested the trip. Take the child away somewhere, she'd said. Away from all this. The whispers. The eyes that looked away, then back, recomposed into an expression of adopted benevolence. The how-*are*-you's that don't want a truthful answer. One month now, of waking up alone. Without the bulky presence of his soft body next to hers, absorbing the nightly news. Without his hand to warm the small of her back when they followed the waiter to a table at their favourite Italian place. Without his laugh, especially the one that came from somewhere deep in his gut and only surfaced when Carrie was around. A month of arrangements and administration, heartbreakingly mundane. The adrenaline that had carried her through had slowed to a drip.

When Kelly wants to surrender to the crashing violence of green waves, to let them swallow her whole until there's nothing left but a straggle of dirty-blond seaweed, she stops. She releases the breath she's trapped. She closes her eyes, pauses, opens them again and orders a mojito from the cute shirtless bartender and pretends she doesn't notice that look from the couple with their guidebooks spread open on the bar who are judging her because it's not yet noon. She smiles as she feels the warm grains beneath her feet, the cleansing drink in her hand. She lets the lime and sugar and rum slide down her throat. She chews on a piece of mint.

She avoids asking questions. Especially the biggest one, which hangs two inches in front of her lips. She swats the whys away like flies.

She tries not to think about Keith. About the time, at a place like this, he bought pink and orange Bermuda shorts, glorious in their ugliness, that rendered a cartoon version of his usual black-clad self. Carrie coaxing them into chocolate chip cookie dough ice cream cones and rounds of Pac-Man at the beachside arcade. Carrie cartwheeling down the beach into the fog. Carrie beaming at the two of them, taking Kelly and Keith's hands and fitting them together.

She tries not to think about how easily Keith tanned. Sunscreen was for wusses, he'd bragged. But the sun was stronger than him. The worst burn of his life, he'd moaned afterward as Kelly applied the aloe vera. She awoke in the night, the sheets slick with aloe, the sound of his ragged breath, the sweet smell of salt drifting through the open window, Carrie's slim white form in a pool of moonlight on the cot in the corner.

Their first evening, she and Carrie go to dinner. Table for two. The breeze licks Kelly's bare shoulders. She orders grilled calamari, garden salad and a glass of white. Carrie has a bowl of vegetable bow-tie pasta. Kelly notices the perfect teeth of the man sitting alone at the next table. Like Keith's. Pure white, straight, square, strong enamel, no stains.

Kelly could tell a lot about someone from their teeth. Stains show overconsumption of wine or coffee. Discoloured roots indicate use of a particular brand of birth control. Erosion, maybe an eating disorder. She could take one look and approximate a personality: stressed caffeine and alcohol-guzzling grinder, or meditative mellow yogi. Inattentive let-things-fly type, or meticulous tooth-care zealot.

Keith's teeth were almost too perfect. She wondered what he was hiding. Just one thing: a small, tiny fracture in his left molar. She told him she could fix it, the first time they met, him in the chair looking up at her from behind cheap plastic goggles, brown eyes shining in the light. But he said no.

Your teeth are your business card, her professor said in dentistry school. Most people don't think about that when they keep their floss hidden in the back of the cabinet until the day of their dentist appointment. White, unstained teeth can take five years off a person's age, increase their attractiveness by 20 per cent.

When she and Keith went out for the first time, she added five years to the age she thought he was while he dipped chips into salsa.

She'd taken a shot of rum before leaving her apartment. She hadn't been on a date since college and she was nervous. Keith kept her wine glass full of sangria and plied her with questions.

"How did you manage to become a dentist by, what, twenty-two?"

Nice try.

She hadn't been ready to tell him her age. Twenty-six, which didn't sound as good as twenty-four or even twenty-five. Some guys want a younger woman on their arm. Plenty of guys in town like that. Guys who'd buy her a vodka cranberry when she went to Sweetwaters and swayed her hips on the dance floor. She accepted because it was a small town and who'd heard of the date rape drug? Small, small talk. Soon as they realized her age, her profession, they bolted. Her teeth mislead them.

Keith, though, he walked her through a surprise June hailstorm and kissed her on the cheek on her front porch as tiny white balls pinged off their heads.

187

The next afternoon at the pool, Carrie plays in the shallow end and Kelly tries not to think about Keith's kiss, the smoothness of his never-chapped lips.

When acquaintances said the things people say at funeral homes, *This too will pass* or *It'll get better* or *I'm so sorry, honey*, she focused on their teeth. How naked it made them. The things she could learn when they opened wide to fit a smoked trout canapé and she could get a better look. She had a practice to maintain, now more than ever, since she couldn't count on Keith. Not even as a patient. By the time he died, Keith's teeth were less than perfect. Fillings, stains from the wine they drank together, the cigarettes he smoked alone. His teeth went downhill as soon as she took him into her care. She saw the hard edge of resentment in his eyes, the pain she was inflicting. She tried not to take those looks personally. She became a dentist in those moments, not a lover. She tried not to let it wear on her, like acid wears down enamel.

It's already getting dark. It's warm here, but the sun still sets early, this close to Christmas. Servers cast long shadows as they light shallow candles on each table. Keith always hated candlelight: the flickering did something to his brain, he said. It made it hard to concentrate. He preferred darkness. She thinks of the time she found him in the kitchen, a still shadow at the sink. She turned on the light and shrieked when she saw his hands covered in blood.

"Don't worry," he lied, "I just broke a glass."

He began lying to her regularly after that. They'd been married three years when he disappeared for the first time. No warning. No note. She wasn't sure who to call. The two of them and the baby the last couple of years. A trio. Sealed and compact. She kept working. Every night, she told herself she wasn't waiting for the phone to ring, but she kept the TV volume so low it was barely audible. She ran a bath for Carrie but then stopped the flow of water in case she'd missed a ring. Used a blow dryer in short bursts. In between, a silence that bred.

When he returned, he rang the doorbell like a visitor. He didn't speak when she opened the door. He'd inherited the cabin after his father's death, he finally told her. He'd needed some time away. He knew he was failing as a father. And as a husband, he added. He loved Carrie almost too fiercely. He couldn't live up to his own standards of fatherhood.

This fatherhood thing, Keith had warned early on, I'm not sure it's for me. I'm not sure I can be responsible for another life. Keith was only ten when his father took the family van and drove it into the St. John River with a bottle of pills in his belly and no intention of coming back. He did come back, though, and maybe that was worse. We're a bunch of fucking depressives, my family, is what Keith said.

Lights out. Once Carrie is settled in bed, Kelly sits in a stiff wicker chair on the balcony overlooking the pool. The rooms with an ocean view had been too expensive.

When Carrie is finally sleeping, Kelly reaches into her suitcase for the bottle of gin wrapped in a pink cashmere sweater that's too hot for this weather. She had an argument with herself before packing the bottle. She won.

The year before Carrie was born, she'd promised Keith she'd stop drinking. She didn't really have a problem. But she drank to compensate, when she felt judged. When she needed the feelings to overflow. That must've bothered him. On the

189

balcony, Kelly tips back a shot. Keith always kept things inside too much, that's why his art never got great. He wasn't willing to put enough of himself into it, embrace radical honesty. Kelly sighs. Radical honesty. That phrase had been running through her head for years, popping up at the strangest of times. Radical honesty, she'd think, when she found a crumpled tissue with lipstick on it in Keith's pants pocket. Radical honesty, she'd think, when another man with a beauty mark near his lips kissed her in an elevator and tasted like stinky cheese. Radical honesty, she'd think, when Keith asked whether she thought he would make a good father.

She'd start to drink and the next thing she knew, she was puking into a stranger's stainless steel kitchen sink at a party. Someone running to get Keith. He'd gather her hair in a ponytail, wipe her face. I'm fine, really. You're not. He'd take her to the bathroom and she'd hide there. She'd wash her ponytail in the sink. She'd muster all her dignity and make her way to the car, fall into the passenger seat, pass out. She'd wake up in bed the next morning, still clothed. Their marriage carried on, like a train that had forgotten its passengers.

After breakfast on their third day, as Carrie splashes in the ocean, Kelly sits under an umbrella's shade and pours some of her gin into an orange juice from the buffet. She eases back into her chair, watches the waves, watches Carrie's breath shudder through her chest as a wave comes up and surprises her. Kelly starts to get up but relaxes when she hears Carrie squeal with laughter.

Carrie was an accident. Pregnancy scared Kelly into submission. Keith rid the house of alcohol and she stayed clean. She felt as pure as she ever had. Feathery. She could barely keep her feet tethered to the ground. Later, she could barely lift them.

Keith became an anxious father even before Carrie was born. He began to go to the cabin alone some weekends. He was teetering. He said that being alone in the woods, hunting, portioning animals with a knife and his hands, made him feel necessary again. It was never easy for him, the part about her having the money. She always had more. But he would always be back on Monday.

That last Monday there was a knock at the door, but it wasn't him. Kelly doubled over in the front hallway like she'd been shot in the stomach. The police officer pressed her head into his chest and she clutched his arm. She lost a day or two to the drugs that were supposed to calm her down. Someone else identified the body. She saw him for the first time when he was scrubbed clean, laid out in a bed of polyester meant to resemble velvet.

At the resort, she can pretend for short stretches that it's just her and Carrie, mother and daughter, an undisturbed unit. But when they get home there'll be much more to contend with: Keith's possessions. On their fourth night, she puts the gin back in its sweater after one more drink. She can have this. She gets into bed beside Carrie and sleeps a dreamless sleep.

By their fifth morning, Carrie's skin is browning, while Kelly's is still as pale as the snow covering their backyard at home. Carrie must get that from her father. Kelly thinks about Carrie growing up looking like him. Will people question them when they go abroad, her with her maiden name and Carrie with his?

Kelly watches a young couple further down the beach. Early twenties, newly in love. The woman's tan accentuated by a black bikini, long auburn-dyed hair that falls to her waist, still unmarred by stretch marks or other signs of age. He has a gym-sculpted six-pack. The types who work on their bodies year round, this one-week vacation to show the fruits of their labour. He rubs lotion into her back like he's scrubbing a floor.

She takes Carrie to that café along the water with the chipped blue paint and yellow-checkered tablecloths. She orders bagels with cream cheese and raspberry jam. When Carrie makes a face, she spreads Carrie's bagel herself and tells her this is what she ate with her mother. Carrie takes a bite and her whole face relaxes in pleasure.

"It's good," she admits, wiping a smear of cream cheese from the corner of her mouth.

"I know," Kelly says.

A man at the next table. Kelly notices him watching the two of them but pretends she doesn't. He's attractive, older but not much, hair with only a suggestion of grey. He has a book in front of him, a cup of coffee but no food. She strains to see the book's spine. He catches her looking. She blushes and he smiles.

She feels reflexively guilty, then gutted. She gathers Carrie and their beach bags and pays in a hurry, races Carrie to the pool.

She sits with a thick paperback she never reads and watches Carrie swim. She opens her eyes in a panic. No one else watching. The weight of this hits her in the stomach and makes her close her eyes again. What was half, now full. No one to share the joy, pain, burden. Carrie flips onto her back and floats, oblivious, eyes closed toward the sun. She looks so peaceful.

On the sixth day, she and Carrie leave the resort and visit the ruins. They climb one hundred and thirty tiny steps to the top of the ancient pyramid. Carrie is thrilled to discover the geckos who roam the wreckage like ancient souls.

"Do they really shed their skin?"

"Yes," Kelly says.

"I wish I could do that," Carrie says.

Kelly wakes that night and finds herself alone in bed. She bolts upright so fast she accidentally scratches her cheek. The room is empty. Then she sees Carrie outside on the balcony in the wicker chair, knees drawn up to her chest and straining against the fabric of her pink nightgown. Kelly moves through the open screen door and trips over a piece of decorative driftwood.

"Carrie?"

Carrie finally turns, her wet face glistening in the reflected light from the pool.

"Why would he do that?" Carrie asks.

"I don't think we'll ever know for sure, honey."

Kelly wants to say more, but Carrie nods, wipes her nose with her hand, walks past Kelly and gets back into bed, facing the wall. Kelly stands in the darkness for a long time before finally getting back into bed beside her.

She takes Carrie to the beach one last time. The sun behind grey clouds, a breeze. Carrie sits patiently on the towel Kelly lays out for her. If Carrie is indulging her, she doesn't show it.

"Sandwich?"

Carrie shakes her head and tears into the Skittles instead, looks at Kelly with a dare.

Radical honesty, Kelly thinks.

"Honey."

"Mom."

Her tone, her too-wise green eyes. It was a mistake, not taking her to the funeral. She can't shield Carrie from this.

Carrie arranges Skittles into a rainbow.

"Honey, I want to talk to you."

"I know, Mom."

Kelly doesn't hide her tears this time.

"Finally," Carrie says.

"Finally what?"

"You're crying."

Carrie curls up against her, feeds her Skittles. They taste unbearably sugary, but she chews them anyway.

Disposed

Sometimes I think about that time when we were sixteen. You said you'd found something. Something important. You wouldn't tell me over the phone. I had to come over. When I arrived, you were on the grass in the backyard.

"Look," you pointed. "It's a new constellation. I just discovered it. I'm calling it Roxana's Belt."

Do you remember? It was an old joke of ours, renaming the constellations. It was weak, that one, so I knew something was up. But you wouldn't tell me. Finally I threatened to leave, and you relented.

"I'll tell you if you lie down," you said.

So I lay beside you in the grass. We both looked up at the stars.

That's when you rolled over and kissed me.

"That's what I wanted to show you," you said.

I've never told Jake about that kiss. I'm sure it would thrill him, to know I once kissed a girl. It seemed like something I should keep for myself.

Would you believe me if I told you it was still the best kiss I've ever had?

Jake doesn't know I write. He doesn't know that when he goes out at night I sit up here and write in this little notebook. Sometimes I used to bring a glass of wine with me, but mostly it was gin. Straight up, on ice. I find it goes down slower than wine, keeps me from getting woozy. There's something about gin that feels clean, botanical. Not like a vice. He'd probably think I was writing all about him, wouldn't he? And today maybe I am, but in general he features surprisingly little in these pages. The neighbour woman, though, she turns up a lot. I see her through the window.

Earlier she was yelling at her kids. *I know you're not retarded*, she said. *I know because I've never gotten a phone call from a teacher saying that you do anything but listen. And yet. Every. Single. Day. Whining, screaming, nonsense.* She ends her tirade by threatening them with boarding school. When I'm a mother, will I also become such a cliché? Will I be able to think of more imaginative threats?

Jake thinks the neighbour is hot. Not that he's ever said as much, but I see the look in his eyes when she goes by with her short shorts, her pink cleavage-baring tank top, her glittery kitten heels. You know those shirts you buy, somewhere like Vegas, white with "Sexy" written on it in pink sequins? She's the type to wear it unironically. Something I might have worn in high school, actually, but that was so long ago.

I always write up here in the attic, on the paisley spread on this spare bed. Cloudy comes too, although I have to carry him up the steps. He likes to curl up on the pillow beside me. Protecting me? ("You're the man of the house now," Jake told Cloudy before leaving for the weekend. "Take care of her, okay?" "That's horrible," I told Jake.)

Sometimes I pretend I'm writing to you. You used to encourage me to keep a journal. You said it was the best way to keep from embarrassing yourself: get it out on paper before it regurgitates in life. Advice that would seem smart to self-conscious teen girls. I never did back then, but I took it up after we stopped being friends. You'd be shocked if you could see me now, trust me. It's not like we imagined, back in school. I am not living in New York City, writing romance novels and shopping at Prada, dating a Jared Leto look-alike with Kurt Cobain sunglasses. I bet you didn't become a Rockette, either. I didn't want to tell you your legs weren't long enough.

People used to say you were stuck up, but I knew better. Just like you knew I wasn't a slut like they said. You knew I hadn't even slept with a boy yet. And that it would be ages before I did.

My body betrayed me, when Jake asked. The blush, my curse. It starts around my chest, red splotches like hives except not hives, and spreads up my neck like an unwanted colony of the fastest kind of ant waving little red flags. If I'm at all anxious, even considering saying anything that isn't the absolute truth, there it is. This is a serious hazard in the real estate business, so I have to wear turtlenecks or scarves to work. So you see why I can't lie to Jake, not now, not ever. Scarves don't fool him: he knows how to unravel me.

I can never remember the medical name for it, this condition, so I just call it hives, even if they aren't, technically, hives. You know that expression, wearing your heart on your sleeve? Well. The embarrassment of going through a door that's held open only to realize it's being held open for someone else. A bloodstain on the back of your dress. Finding someone waiting outside the bathroom when you've just passed a lot of gas. Your mother-in-law doing your laundry thinking she's doing you a favour and finding the too-sexy lingerie your husband bought you as a joke. It's worse than all that. And of course, the embarrassment of the hives themselves only makes them spread, multiply like pre-teen boys around a hidden Playboy at sleep-away camp.

So when Jake said, "I thought you were on the pill," I didn't stand a chance against my body. Its truth.

So small, what I did. A flick of the wrist; the pack of pills, disposed. The bin in our shared bathroom, the powdery blue one off the bedroom. Jake takes the garbage out every Tuesday and Friday, and he always empties the bathroom garbage. So I knew he saw it. And we'd silently agreed to try, just this once, to see what happened.

My hair stylist, Maria, told me that immediately after you go off the pill is the best time. Your body is pumped, plump, primed.

It worked.

Right now, I'm sure, he is telling his friends about how I tricked him. They're in upstate New York, camping (glamping, actually) and drinking obscene amounts of expensive scotch. Christie always buys a bottle of Johnnie Walker Blue Label to send with Ryan, her way of making nice. She must sense the psychic sneers the guys otherwise send in her direction. Honestly, I don't know why she wastes her money—those guys would drink Drano, most of them. Except then, not to be outdone by Ryan, the runt of the litter, the other guys feel they have to bring something to keep up. This year, Jake brought a Japanese single malt that was recently named best whiskey in the world, a first for Japan.

Jake isn't a big drinker, and by that I mean he doesn't drink often. But when he does drink he is a big drinker, and that's when his tongue loosens. It's 10 P.M. and surely he's three-quarters of the way into the bottle. By now he's told them the news and has insinuated his lack of involvement in the planning of said news.

Despite what he says, I wasn't trying to trick him. Jake doesn't know what's good for him. He wants to be a daddy, I know he does, but his goofball big-kid-in-adult-clothing Adam Sandler schtick makes that hard to admit. He needed a hand getting into the role, like a dog that needs to be thrown into the lake to learn how to swim. Those guys, they may think they know him, but I'm the one who knows Jake best.

All those other guys already have kids and Jake's not one to be left behind, so really, what were we waiting for? We've been married three years already. We had a chocolate fountain at our wedding. There were gifts (well, a pile of cash), assumptions. Those guys, with their kids, they're not going to be sympathetic to Jake's resistance. Except maybe Simon, the last bachelor type in the group. But even he finally got married last year. I guess it still counts even though it was a civil ceremony at city hall— Jake's still pissed that we weren't invited—and apparently she didn't wear a white dress.

Jake says I bottle things up too much.

For example: it shouldn't have bothered me when you, my ex-best friend, a girl I haven't spoken to since we parted ways at the end of the twelfth grade in the dramatic fashion only teenagers can muster, posted her sonogram on Facebook. You made some inside jokey reference to your husband not being allowed to name the baby after a *Lord of the Rings* character. I had admired your restraint in the past, everything you did not post on Facebook. Your profile was trim, elegant almost. But this? This was full-throttle in the opposite direction.

I promised myself long ago that when I got pregnant, there would be no such post. A sonogram is for the parents alone: no one else wants to see your little white blob and feel obligated to say something about it.

So why should it bother me, this sonogram? I was counting the ones who weren't yet pregnant. And you were one of them. One of the few. Someone to measure myself by. I was able to tell myself: at least *she* hasn't gotten pregnant yet either.

Is it biological, this competitiveness? Hard-wired?

But, I admit, there may have been other factors at play, in your case. When you got pregnant? That's when I knew it was too late, and I had to seal my fate.

So I threw out the pills.

I turned thirty-five this year. It's a painful age: not yet too late, not late enough to simply give up and be done with it, but getting closer and closer to the cusp. A different classification of pregnancy among the docs. And I felt my infertility approaching, hat in hand, like those gunshots I hear in the distance. It's been less than a year since we moved here from the city, Jake and I, and I'm still not used to the gunshots that signal something feral, lurking yet far off. Dangerous. Violent. What are they shooting at?

We know things before we think we know them, a bodily knowledge that starts deep in the bones, and I know Jake knew. And so what is he saying to the guys right now? That I tricked him, like a little witch? That now he feels the shackles of impending fatherhood coming for him, the same way I feel the infertility and the gunshots?

Maybe, by now, Jake is in the woods, puking. He never could hold his liquor. Even on our wedding night, I found him in the toilet at the end of the night. And he never learns, never tempers his drinking to compensate. Luckily, he doesn't drink often.

Jake suggested I do something with myself this weekend, too. Take a trip with some girlfriends. I pretended to consider it to save us both the embarrassment, rather than acknowledging what we both know, deep down: I don't have any friends. Sure, I have "friends," acquaintances, people I chat with at spinning class or at the clay café where I make misshapen mugs on rainy afternoons. The real estate market is all sewn up around here and I haven't been able to get a job since we moved. Hence the spinning classes, the pottery, the frequent trips to the nail salon.

There's no one with whom I have enough intimacy to suggest a trip. Maybe Jake thinks that's why I threw out the pills: loneliness. But I know a baby won't solve that. Besides, say what you will about equality, but let's be honest: once you start having babies, a guys' weekend is a hell of a lot easier to organize than even a girls' night out. Jake's known those guys since university and they get on a plane once a year to meet each other. And since moving here, Jake's also made friends at the golf course. Now he meets them for a round every Saturday and they go for beers afterward. It's easier for men, isn't it?

The thing about the neighbour woman, I suppose, is that she doesn't seem to have inhibitions. Wears and says what she wants, no thought toward consequences. I see her out there now, yelling at her husband. She gets it off her chest, and then it's gone. Then she's free.

Regarding the loneliness: let's not forget Cloudy. I don't know who gave him that name; he's a rescue. Everyone around our new town loves Cloudy. No one knows my name, but they sure know his. He's small and black, svelte and lean with velvet-soft floppy ears and a patch of regal white on his chest. Huge puppy eyes that follow you. A tail that wags furiously when anyone so much as glances in his direction. In other words: adorable. He's a people dog who craves affection. He'll prod you politely with his paw or stick his wet nose into the palm of your hand and push it up onto his head. He'll press himself against you, lean his head into your hand. So trusting.

Most dogs around here are huge, imposing, meant more as guard dogs than pets. People don't bring them around to the farmer's market and the food co-op, like we do Cloudy. All the other dogs bark at Cloudy when we pass on our walks, on the country road where a neighbour finally gave me some neighbourly advice and told me to walk on the side facing traffic, so I could see what's coming.

"The way people drive around here," he said. "That way you won't have to keep looking over your shoulder."

People here leave their dogs off leash, so the dogs lope up to greet Cloudy and me. Each time one of these big dogs approach, Cloudy's little fear patch at the base of his neck sticks up and he looks like a little dinosaur puppy. I smooth it down when I can. I understand how he feels, his body betraying his emotions like that. I don't let Cloudy off leash. Still a city girl, a city dog, I guess. Also, I still pick up the poop. No one else out here seems to.

Cloudy barks a lot more in the country than he did in the city. The gunshots make him bark especially frantically. We had a run-in with another owner and his big dog the other day, and with Cloudy's fear patch that then brought out my hives, perhaps it's no wonder we have no friends. We're both having a hard time settling in.

Jake says I over-explain. Like how if someone asks what kind of dog Cloudy is, I can't just say he's a rat terrier. I have to say we think he's a rat terrier but mixed with what we don't know, because we got him through a rescue organization. People want simple answers, says Jake. Especially here.

It's easy to judge people when you have a cute little dog by your side. The ones who look right through him, like the neighbour woman did, no reaction? Wow. If I ever have to go out without Cloudy, it's like I'm missing my divining rod. How to know? Can you really ever know a person before you see how they interact with your dog? I read somewhere that once you have a child, your dog becomes a pet. I tell Cloudy that won't happen to him. But what if I don't love this baby as much as I love Cloudy?

Do you remember how we used to lie on your bed, side by side, reading a book? You always got to choose the book. I often had to reread the same book at home to keep up. I was too conscious of you there beside me to focus on the words in front of me, even if it was just *Sweet Valley High*. I didn't even like those books, but I had to keep up with the plot in case you wanted to talk about it.

It would have been too typical for me to hate your boyfriend when you got one, so I chose to befriend him instead. Your parents were strict, and when you couldn't come out he came to pick me up instead, always in his red Jeep. Did you know about that? He bought the Jeep at the used car dealer down the street from my house. I was with him, not you.

203

Would you believe me if I told you I don't remember why we stopped speaking? I truly don't. Was it about that boyfriend, whose name I can't even remember? About the time I threw a conniption fit over the dark hair growing on my upper lip, in the downstairs bathroom where your mother could hear me and decide I was a bad influence, too vain? Or was it that you saw something deep inside me, something that was hidden to everyone else? If that was it, please let me in on the secret. Self-awareness has never been my strong suit. All these years I've assumed it was you who stopped speaking to me. But by now I've also learned that my memory is terribly unreliable. What if it was me who stopped speaking to you?

When I saw your sonogram, I didn't like it, like all the others did. But I didn't click block, either, which my therapist would surely tell me is the mentally healthy thing to do. I thought about that kiss, an intensity I'll never have again, the pretty Marilyn Monroe mole near your lips. And I had to remind myself that was a very, very long time ago.

"What's wrong with you?" you'd asked me that night, touching a finger to a red splotch on my collarbone, another on my neck.

I should have explained, but instead I drew away as the hives multiplied, too young to channel emotions into logical phrases, into syllables passing my lips. Too embarrassed by bodily truths.

Jake and his friends: by now I bet they're all passed out, except Simon. You know that game you play? Come on, don't tell me you've never played it. If I had to sleep with one of my husband's friends, only because my life depended on it, who would I choose? Well, I choose Simon.

Simon is the one who can hold his liquor. Simon eats at restaurants where they clean the crumbs off the table and serve mint sorbet between courses. Simon doesn't have any rugrats scuffing his hardwood or crayoning the walls or giving him teabags for under eyes. Simon still has a six-pack, no dad bod on him. Jake has a dad bod despite his until recent status as a non-dad and even now he can't yet call it a dad bod because they say to wait until thirteen weeks before you refer to yourselves as parents.

I knew a man who lost weight by eating an avocado every day. He swore off meat and focused on things like chickpeas and mung beans. Miso dressings. It didn't take long. The pounds melted away. I've told Jake about this but he doesn't listen. He insists on eating lunch at Pizza Hut, day in and day out. It's closest to the office, he says, and he can eat with one hand while reading emails on his Blackberry with the other. He folds his pizza, New-York-style. Once in a while he mixes things up and goes to Papa John's.

Do you think I tricked him? Would you have done what I did, if you had to?

Do you ask lots of leading questions, as Jake says I do? I can't win with you, he likes to say. How many other husbands around the world are saying that right now? I tell him he can win by cleaning the tiny little hairs out of the sink after he trims his beard. I clean them myself, most of the time, but sometimes I find more days later, when I go to clean behind the faucet. Proof of his manliness, Jake says.

I don't tell him about waxing my upper lip. Proof of my manliness? He once told me that most women would kill to have hairless arms like mine and I still didn't speak up. A woman has to keep her secrets.

What are your secrets? What kind of mother are you? By now you can call yourself a mother, I'm sure of it, even if I haven't seen any other posts since the sonogram. That was months ago, and I wonder why you've stopped posting.

Without Jake here, Cloudy barks more often. Even more often than in our regular country life, which is more often than in our city life. I'm not sure if he feels protective of me, or just less secure without Jake here. Maybe he's not confident in my ability to keep him safe. Right now, as I'm writing this, he's rushed downstairs (funny how he'll run down the stairs but not up them) and is barking his paws off. I could go down, but I know I'll find nothing, like I always do. Nothing.

But maybe it's something? I could go downstairs to check, but I've gotten myself in just the right writing position, and I still have half a glass of lemonade (because, sadly, of course I've had to give up the gin) and melted ice left.

What if I were to hear a noise, something too human to be Cloudy? A thief. What if I were to hear the slow slide of a drawer opening, clearly the thief going through my underwear, because isn't that what they all do? Do they keep the stolen goods in their own underwear drawer at home? Or discard them once the thrill is over?

If the footsteps started coming up the stairs, if I felt my life in danger, would my thoughts turn to Jake, to the easy laugh I've always loved, to the way he rubs his hands together when he's excited? To our unborn baby, still unnamed? To Cloudy, the way he curls up in the crook of my legs and rests his head on my knee? To you, the way your voice cracked in half when you said my name as I was leaving that night, the blank face you presented me with afterward, like nothing had happened? Or simply how to save myself? Would I tell the thief I was pregnant? Would that save me? I don't have any proof to show him—it's too early for a sonogram. Would you use your baby as a shield, if a murderer broke into your house?

ACKNOWLEDGEMENTS

Big thanks to my editor Dimitri Nasrallah, my publisher Simon Dardick, and everyone at Véhicule Press for their support of this book. Thank you to the Quebec Writers' Federation, especially my mentor Elise Moser, under whose guidance many of these stories first took shape. Working with Jessica Grant at the Piper's Frith writer's retreat provided crucial inspiration.

"Rabbits with Red Eyes" appeared in *carte blanche*. A previous version of "Out Taming Horses" appeared in *Eclectica*. An earlier version of "How To Be A Widow" appeared in *Tupelo Quarterly*. Thanks to the editors of those publications for supporting my work. I am grateful to the Conseil des arts et des lettres du Québec for its financial support.

Many thanks to the friends whose support and conversation gave me the sustenance to keep writing. For invaluable feedback on early drafts, I am indebted to Nisha Coleman, Michelle Syba, Virginia Konchan, Nathaniel Penn, Pamela Casey, David Koloszyc, and Teri Vlassopoulos.

Much gratitude to Caroline, Teri, and my family for their continual support. To Midnight, who has quite literally been by my side through so much writing and editing, and to Kenneth, for everything.

ESPLANADE
Books

THE FICTION IMPRINT AT VÉHICULE PRESS

A House by the Sea : A novel by Sikeena Karmali
A Short Journey by Car : Stories by Liam Durcan
Seventeen Tomatoes : Tales from Kashmir : Stories by Jaspreet Singh
Garbage Head : A novel by Christopher Willard
The Rent Collector : A novel by B. Glen Rotchin
Dead Man's Float : A novel by Nicholas Maes
Optique : Stories by Clayton Bailey
Out of Cleveland : Stories by Lolette Kuby
Pardon Our Monsters : Stories by Andrew Hood
Chef : A novel by Jaspreet Singh
Orfeo : A novel by Hans-Jürgen Greif
[Translated from the French by Fred A. Reed]
Anna's Shadow : A novel by David Manicom
Sundre : A novel by Christopher Willard
Animals : A novel by Don LePan
Writing Personals : A novel by Lolette Kuby
Niko : A novel by Dimitri Nasrallah
Stopping for Strangers : Stories by Daniel Griffin
The Love Monster: A novel by Missy Marston
A Message for the Emperor : A novel by Mark Frutkin
New Tab : A novel by Guillaume Morissette
Swing in the House : Stories by Anita Anand
Breathing Lessons : A novel by Andy Sinclair
Ex-Yu : Stories by Josip Novakovich

The Goddess of Fireflies : A novel by Geneviève Pettersen
[Translated from the French by Neil Smith]
All That Sang : A novella by Lydia Perović
Hungary-Hollywood Express : A novel by Éric Plamondon
[Translated from the French by Dimitri Nasrallah]
Tumbleweed : Stories by Josip Novakovich
Sun of a Distant Land : A novel by David Bouchet
[Translated from the French by Claire Holden Rothman]
A Three-Tiered Pastel Dream : Stories by Lesley Trites

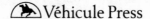 Véhicule Press